wondergirls™

Team Player

Jillian Brooks

SCHOLASTIC INC.

New York Toronto London Auckland Sydney
Mexico City New Delhi Hong Kong Buenos Aires

ISBN 0-439-35490-0

Produced by 17th Street Productions,
an Alloy, Inc. company
151 West 26th Street
New York, NY 10001

chapter
ONE

Ten Things I Must Do Before the End of Sixth Grade

1.   Win the state soccer championship.

2.   Wear purple eye shadow.

3.   Meet Shauna Ferris.

4.   Get my mom to let me get highlights.

5.   Throw the best party ever!

6.   Get "mystery meat loaf" banned from the cafeteria on Wednesdays.

7.   Make National Junior Honor Society.

8.   Do better in English.

9.   Have a boyfriend.

10.   Get voted captain of the soccer team.

"Has anybody seen my lucky plate?" I asked.

It was eight o'clock on Monday morning, and I was staring at a cabinet full of wheat-bran flakes and oat-free oatmeal. I didn't even know that was possible. What I did know was that I definitely did not want to go to my first soccer practice at my new school without eating breakfast on my lucky plate.

"Dad, have you seen it?" I asked hopefully.

"Sorry, honey," Dad answered without looking up. He had his nose buried in a huge stack of papers. My dad is Wonder Lake's most successful real estate lawyer. I guess it doesn't hurt that he's six-foot-four with piercing blue eyes and this really serious expression on his face. He kind of intimidates people. But with me he's just a big softie.

Mom was on her cell phone to her assistant. "I'll meet you at the courthouse at eight-thirty," she said, smiling at me. Mom has a great smile. She's a lawyer, too, but she could've been a model. People say I look like her. We have the same auburn hair and green eyes.

"Mom, have you seen my soccer plate?" I whispered. Without missing a beat, she pointed at the dishwasher. I opened it up and pulled out my plate. It was smeared with day-old cream cheese.

"Gross," I said, wrinkling my nose.

Mom put her hand over her free ear so she could concentrate on her phone call. "Yes. Let's set the arraignment for Tuesday."

She was so distracted, she emptied three packets of Equal into her coffee. I knew that in a minute, she'd take a sip and make a face and blame the coffeemaker. My parents are really focused when it comes to work. It's me they have a hard time seeing clearly sometimes.

I took a sponge to my dirty plate and rinsed it clean. "Mom? What's for breakfast?" I asked.

She put her hand over the mouthpiece. "Honey, check the pantry. There's food in there. Yes, Monica, I'm still here."

Hello? I thought. *I'm still here, too.*

Whatever.

In the pantry I managed to find a whole-wheat English muffin. It wasn't a Pop-Tart, but it would do. Mom is a big health freak, and there's never anything edible in the house. Personally, I would've sold my brother for a Twinkie. Too bad I don't have a brother. Or a sister. I'm an only child. It's just me, Mom, Dad, and our housekeeper, Anya.

It would get kind of lonely if I didn't have one best friend: Amanda Kempner, and two kind-of best friends: Felicia Fiol and Traci McClintic. Amanda and I have been superclose since we were little. We even lived on the same street till my parents moved to a bigger house last year. Felicia and I met over the summer and hit it off right away. And Traci just moved to Wonder Lake from Charleston, South Carolina. She is supposed to be my relief player on the soccer team, but I didn't plan to give her any reason to play. Center forward was my position, and I wanted to own it.

The four of us had already started making a name for ourselves at our new school—Wonder Lake Middle School. Over the weekend we'd thrown a party—a fund-raiser for the animal shelter Felicia's dad runs—and half the kids at school had shown up. It was a big success. Everybody would probably still be talking about it at school today. I couldn't wait to hear our names in the hallways. We were only in sixth grade, but together we were going to rule the school.

Mom took a sip of coffee and spit it back in her china cup. "Oh, that's awful. There must be something wrong with the coffeemaker."

I couldn't help laughing. "*Mom*," I said. "Hello? You just put three packets of *chemicals* in your coffee."

"I did? Oh, my goodness." Mom shook her head. She patted the top of my head like I was still in first grade, totally messing up my hair.

Dad had out his red pen and was slashing away at the contract he was reading the way my English teacher, Mrs. Scott, marked up my last quiz. English was turning out to be my worst subject, and my quizzes kept coming back with big red X's on them. The sight of the red pen made me shudder. I tried to think about something good.

"Dad," I said through a mouthful of muffin. "Don't forget I've got soccer practice till five-thirty today."

"How could I forget to pick up the new star of the Wonder Lake Muskrats?" Dad said. He gave me a quick wink.

"Dad," I said, rolling my eyes. "I'm not the star yet."

"But you will be. I know the Lightnings will miss you this year."

The Lightnings were my old team at the private all-girls school I went to until I switched to WLMS. I was lower-school captain for the Lightnings, and one day I wanted to be captain of the Muskrats. Today was the team's first practice and a chance for me to show Coach Talbot and all the other girls what I could do. I pushed my lucky plate aside, ready to start the day.

"Shouldn't we be going, Mom?" I asked.

Mom looked at her watch. "Honey, we've still got ten minutes. No, not you, Monica. Sorry," she said into the phone.

Ten minutes? It felt like forever. With a sigh I reached for the newspaper and flipped it open to the Lifestyles page. I stopped cold. Smack in the middle of the page was a huge ad announcing that the music store in the mall was throwing a party for the release of Shauna Ferris's new CD. They were actually giving away free, signed Shauna T-shirts to the first twenty-five people in line. This was huge! Shauna Ferris was my absolute favorite singer in the whole world, and there was no way I was missing out on a signed T-shirt.

There was just one small problem. The T-shirts were being given out at four o'clock—the same time as soccer practice.

Okay, so maybe it was a big problem.

I couldn't miss my first soccer practice. It was crucial. But so was getting a signed one-of-a-kind Shauna Ferris T-shirt.

Mom finished her phone call and grabbed her keys and purse. "Okay," she said. "If you want to go a little early, I can take you now, sweetie."

"Thanks, Mom," I said. My lucky soccer plate seemed to stare back at me. So did the ad in the paper. I covered my plate with the paper.

On the ride to school I made my plan. I'd tell Coach Talbot I wasn't feeling well and that I'd make up the practice later in the week. Then I'd be free to take the bus to the mall and be back in time for my dad to pick me up at five-thirty. It could work. It *had* to work.

"Here we are," Mom said as we pulled up in front of the school. Someone had changed the gold letters on the big blue sign over the weekend. It now read: WONDER LAKE MIDDLE SCHOOL. HOME OF THE GIRLS STATE SOCCER CHAMPS. GO, MUSKRATS! Our team had a lot to live up to. My throat tightened.

"Arielle? Are you okay?" Mom asked with a concerned frown.

"Sure, just a little nervous," I said. I hoped I didn't look guilty. As a lawyer and a mom, she could really sniff out guilt.

"Don't worry, sweetheart—give it time. I bet you'll

be just as popular here as you were at Wonder Lake Academy."

Mom didn't get that it wasn't school I was worried about—it was soccer. Or the soccer I was going to miss when I skipped practice. Her being so nice only made me feel even more guilty.

"I better go," I said, bolting from the car. Felicia and Traci waved to me from the school's big stone steps.

"Dad will pick you up at five-thirty," Mom called after me, like I was a little kid who'd forgotten her lunch box or something. I hoped nobody had heard her. How embarrassing.

"I love your outfit," Felicia said as I walked up. Her long black curls looked extra bouncy today.

"Thanks. I like yours, too," I said, taking in her orange-striped rugby shirt and white jeans. "Hey, I have those same jeans."

"I know," Felicia said. "They looked so good on you, I just had to get a pair."

Traci looked down at her plain blue sneakers. She and Felicia used to spend summers together before Felicia's parents got divorced the year before last. I think when Traci moved here, she expected to have Felicia all to herself. She wasn't used to sharing her. And whenever Felicia and I shared a private joke or wore the same barrettes on the same day, Traci gave us funny looks.

"Where's Amanda?" I asked, changing the subject.

"She's taking down the All for Paws posters that were in some of the hallways," Traci answered. All for Paws was the name of our weekend fund-raiser.

A couple of girls who'd been at the party waved to me on their way up the steps.

"Great party, Arielle," a blond girl named Callie said.

Her friend smiled at me. "Yeah, it was a ton of fun. When's your next one?"

"I'll keep you posted," I said.

I was so glad my party had been a big hit, even if I'd had to share it with a bunch of dogs and cats.

"There are lots of animals that still need good homes. Why don't y'all—I mean, you—stop by the shelter sometime?" Traci reminded them.

Of course, she just had to get it in about the animals and make sure no one thought the party was my idea. Whatever.

Traci had promised to wait for Amanda, so Felicia and I walked through the dark hallways of Wonder Lake Middle School on our way to homeroom. The building was pretty old, with heavy wooden beams overhead. The lockers were practically antiques: I had to hit mine a couple of times to get it to open. My last school had been really modern. But it was small, we had to wear uniforms, and there weren't any boys. I was definitely ready for a change.

"Did you hear about the Shauna Ferris giveaway at the mall today?" Felicia asked.

"I'm going," I blurted.

"Oh, my gosh! You are? For real?" Felicia's eyes got huge.

"Sure," I answered. "Want to come with me?"

Felicia tossed her dark curls over her shoulders. "I wish I could. I have to help out in my mom's bakery after school. She's showing me how to decorate the birthday cakes."

"Bummer," I said. Since Felicia's parents were divorced, she split her time between her dad's house and her mom's.

The bell rang.

"I wish I had homeroom with the three of you instead of being stuck in Mr. Reid's class." Felicia sighed.

"Yeah. I can't believe he actually made you do book reports. Isn't it against the rules to have homework in homeroom?" I asked.

"It should be," Felicia said, stopping at her classroom door. "Well, see you later."

I headed down the hall to Ms. McClintic's homeroom. It was too bad that Felicia couldn't come to the mall with me, but I couldn't wait to spring the news on Amanda. She was a Shauna fan, too, and I just knew she'd flip about the T-shirts.

Just then Amanda and Traci came in and parked

themselves right behind me. Our ditsy teacher, Ms. McClintic, wasn't big on seating charts, thank goodness, so we got to sit together every day.

"Hey," Amanda whispered. "I got all the posters down and put them in the recycling bins by the office." She had paired a tie-dyed T-shirt with a long, flowy skirt and some Mardi Gras beads. It was totally Amanda.

"Thanks for taking care of the cleanup," I whispered back.

"No problemo," she said.

I wanted to tell her about the Shauna giveaway, but Ms. McClintic paced in front of the chalkboard, going on and on about a new "project." Oh, no. I hoped she hadn't been talking to Mr. Reid in the faculty lounge. Between all my classes and soccer, I had enough on my plate. I didn't need homeroom homework.

"I think this will be a great way for all of us to get to know one another," Ms. McClintic said, searching through her desk. She backed up against the chalkboard, covering her butt in white, dusty chalk.

"Has anyone seen my pen?" she asked.

Traci crouched low in her chair. Her cheeks turned red. "You stuck it behind your ear," she whispered loudly.

Ms. McClintic patted her frizzy hair and found the missing pen. "Oh, thank you, honey."

Ms. McClintic is Traci's mom, and Traci cringes every time she calls her "honey." Can you blame her?

Another teacher knocked on the door to speak to Ms. McClintic about something. While she was outside, I turned around to give Amanda the news about the Shauna T-shirts.

"So what do you think?" I asked. "Are you totally excited? We can catch the bus right on the corner, go to the mall and get our T-shirts, and my dad will pick us up here at five-thirty." I left out the part about skipping practice and fibbing to my parents. There's no way Amanda would go with me if she knew about that. It felt weird holding something back, though. I always tell Amanda everything.

"Sounds amazing," she said. Her smile turned to a frown. "The thing is, I sort of promised Felicia's dad that I'd come help out at the animal shelter today. He rescued a new puppy named Grits, and I hear he's the cutest thing ever!"

Okay. I admit it. I'm not an animal nut. In third grade, when every other girl was reading horse books and playing with unicorn dolls, I was stealing my mom's *Vogue*. Besides, I couldn't believe that Amanda would pass up a once-in-a-lifetime chance to go to the CD party. We'd probably be the only girls in school with those shirts. How cool would that be?

"Look," I said, a little impatiently. "Can't you go see Grubs another day?"

"It's Grits," Amanda said. Uh-oh. She sounded hurt. Not good.

11

"Okay, whatever. I'm only your best friend. Don't let me keep you from your dog friends, who are obviously more important." I knew I was being kind of a baby, but it wouldn't be half as much fun without her. I really wanted her to come.

Amanda crossed her arms. It was her famous I'm-thinking-it-over pose. "No. I want to go. But only if you promise to help out at the animal shelter sometime."

"Of course," I said, like I'd planned to help out all along. I would've promised to do twelve book reports and read them all out loud if it meant she'd say yes. It was settled. Today at four o'clock Amanda and I would be standing at the front of the line when they handed out the Shauna T-shirts.

"Wait a minute. Arielle, you can't go," Traci piped up. "You have soccer practice after school."

I took a deep breath. *Here goes,* I thought. "Um, well, my dad talked to Coach Talbot about excusing me from practice today, and, um, she said it was okay. I can make it up later," I said. I tried to sound like it was no big deal, but my heart was bouncing all over the place in my chest.

"Yeah, but Arielle . . . it's your first real practice," Amanda reminded me. "You don't want to miss it, do you?"

I shrugged. "You know how the first practice is. Just a big review of drills you learned over the summer and getting to know everybody's name and all."

"You don't know that for sure," Traci said. I wished she would just let it go.

"Traci's right, Arielle. What if you miss something important?" Amanda said.

"I won't," I said, rolling my eyes. Amanda was siding with Traci again. Before Traci had moved here, it had always been Amanda and me, best friends, together forever. Now it was Traci this and Traci that. It was really annoying.

"Look, I already know most of that stuff from soccer camp, anyway," I said, doodling all over my notebook as if to say the discussion was over. Why were my friends acting so weird? It was just one day. How much could they cover in one practice?

"And your dad's going to pick us up?" Amanda asked, eyeing me.

"Five-thirty, on the dot," I chirped. Yes! She was going!

"Okay, I'm in." Amanda gave me a huge smile.

"Cool!" I said. "I can't wait!" I guess I said that part a little too loud.

"Did you have something to share with the class, Arielle?" Ms. McClintic said, coming back into the classroom.

Oops.

"Uh, no, Ms. McClintic. I was just thinking about the assignment you gave us. It sounds great. I just meant that I can't wait to do it." I gave her a winning

13

smile, the one that usually got me a new outfit from my dad or an extra cookie from Anya.

Ms. McClintic looked confused. "But I haven't assigned the project yet, dear," she said.

I was so busted. People started snickering.

In the back of the room Ryan Bradley called, "Earth to Arielle. Come in, Arielle!" Sometimes Ryan could be really funny. And sometimes, like right now, he was just plain annoying.

I glanced back just a little bit—like I couldn't even bother to turn my whole head around and look at him. "So funny, Ryan. Did you think that up all by yourself?"

Two guys sitting next to me laughed.

Traci pulled nervously at her shirt collar. "Well, you did sort of space out, Arielle," she said quietly. I saw her give Ryan a quick look and blush bright red. Oh, brother, I could definitely smell a crush.

"All right," Ms. McClintic said. "Let's get back to business."

I tried to concentrate so I didn't embarrass myself any more. Ms. McClintic handed out stapled questionnaires, starting with me. "This project—for those of you who don't have psychic powers like Arielle—is entitled 'Who Am I?' It's a place for you to write down your feelings, hobbies, likes, dislikes, things you wish you could change about yourself, things you're happy with. There are no right or wrong answers. No grades, unless you don't do it, in which case it's a zero. It's a way for us all to get to know one another." She spread her arms out wide.

I took a look at the first question: *If you were an animal, what kind of animal would you be?* Animals again. Ugh.

"Whoa," I said to Amanda. "This is a little tutti-frutti even for Ms. McClintic."

Traci's head shot up, and I clapped my hand over my mouth. I hadn't meant for her to hear me. I passed her a note.

Sorry, Traci. Me and my big mouth. I drew a little frowny face on it to show I was sorry.

She scribbled back an answer. *That's okay. It is sort of a dumb assignment.*

The bell rang. Felicia ran to meet us outside homeroom, and we walked to class together. On the walls, posters begged us to come out and support the Muskrats in their first match against the Tigers. My stomach did a flip-flop. Our first game was less than three weeks away.

The rest of the day felt like a gazillion years. I couldn't stop thinking about after school. I pictured Amanda and me getting our brand-new Shauna shirts. Then I imagined us walking into the cafeteria tomorrow. Everybody would know we were the coolest sixth graders in school.

But when the last bell rang, there was still something I had to do.

"Wait right here," I said to Amanda at our lockers. "I'll be right back. I just want to remind Coach Talbot that I won't be there today."

I raced down the stairs till I got to the heavy wooden doors of the gym. I went inside and hurried over to the phys-ed office. But it was empty. Where was Coach Talbot? She just had to be there!

"Arielle? You're a little early. Go ahead and suit up," Coach Talbot said, coming up behind me. As usual, she was carrying her clipboard and wearing her silver whistle.

My mouth went completely dry. "I, uh, I mean . . . Coach Talbot?"

"Yes, Arielle?" Her brows knitted together, and she cocked her head. "Are you okay?"

"Yes. I mean, no." Words started flying out of my mouth. "I don't feel well. It's my stomach." I held my hand over my stomach. "I think it was something I ate. I'm sorry, but I have to miss practice."

Coach Talbot put her arm around my shoulders. "Do you need to go see the nurse? I could walk you over there. . . ."

"No!" I practically shouted. "I think I'd better go straight home. My friend Amanda is going to take me."

"Okay," she said. "I'll put Traci in your position today. Maybe the two of you can get together and

16

go over the drills tomorrow if you're feeling better."

"Thanks, Coach Talbot."

"Hope you do feel better," she called after me.

For the first time I really did feel sick . . . about lying. When I ran back upstairs, Amanda was standing next to my locker.

"Ready?" she asked.

"Totally!" I said. I quickly opened my locker and grabbed my dreaded English book and stuffed it in my bag.

One of the girls from the soccer team waved to me from the other end of the hall. I felt like there was a huge Guilty sign on my forehead. I wanted out of there fast.

"Come on, Amanda. We better go," I said, tugging at her sleeve. With Amanda right behind me, I raced for the back doors and the bus stop, praying I didn't run into Coach Talbot or anyone else along the way.

chapter
TWO

Horoscope

ARIES, March 19–April 18. Your day today: Make good investments with your time. What seems like a great deal may backfire. Honor your responsibilities and all will be well. Wear pink.

"Wait!" Amanda tore her arm away from mine and stopped dead. We were halfway down the sidewalk between the bus stop and the school. "I've got to call my stepmom. I left her a message before, but what if she didn't get it? I'd better call her again and make sure this is okay."

I looked behind us for any sign of Coach Talbot. I was supposed to be sick and on my way home. "Can't you call her from the mall?" I asked nervously.

Amanda shook her head. "No. She'll flip. I have to go back and use the phone in the office."

The office? That was as good as marching behind enemy lines and surrendering. Besides, if we didn't get on the bus soon, we'd get to the mall too late and end up stuck at the back of the line. I didn't want to skip soccer practice *and* not get a T-shirt. But Amanda wasn't budging.

"All right." I sighed. "Let's go."

We stepped through the huge front doors of the school and into the hall that led to the front office. The halls were clearing out. Kids were either out front waiting for buses or rides, or they were in the cafeteria or library or auditorium for various club meetings. I leaned up against the auditorium doors and watched Amanda through the office windows while she called her stepmom.

I got bored and was headed for the water fountain when I saw Coach Talbot coming up the stairs at the end of the hall, her silver whistle swinging from around her neck. For a second I froze. Just the sight of her curly red hair sent new fear through me. But there was nowhere to go. I couldn't go into the office. There was some drama club meeting going on in the library. And I couldn't just stand there in the hallway like a guilty dork, waiting to get caught.

I ducked into the auditorium. A few seconds later I pushed open the doors a tiny bit to sneak a peek. Coach Talbot was right there in front of the office. I hoped she didn't go inside where she could overhear Amanda talking about our plans on the phone. I hadn't felt this nervous since the time I had to recite the Pledge of Allegiance at my first-grade graduation.

"Uh, excuse me. Are you here for the student government meeting?"

I'd been so busy looking out into the hallway, I hadn't stopped to think about what might be going on in the auditorium. I turned around to see a group of about ten seventh and eighth graders staring at me. You might as well have stamped Superdork on my forehead.

"Can I help you?" The voice belonged to a really cute guy with brown hair and big brown eyes.

What could I say? *No thanks, I'm just hiding out from my soccer coach?* "Uh, yeah. Can you tell me the way to the library?"

Lame. Lame. Double lame.

"Sure. It's down the hall at the end. The place with all the books? You can't miss it."

The place with all the books. Right. "Thanks," I said, trying to flash a smile that I hoped made me look sweet and cool at the same time. "Keep up the good work with student government. It's important." Then I actually gave him a thumbs-up. I felt like such a loser.

A few seventh graders snickered, but the guy just smiled. "Okay, thanks," he said.

I didn't know what was worse, being stuck in the auditorium like a loser or running into Coach Talbot. I peeked out into the hallway again, and thankfully, the coast was clear.

Amanda looked puzzled when I met her in front of the office. "Hey, where were you?" she said.

"Never mind," I told her, putting my arm through hers and leading the way. "Let's just *go*."

We ran smack into Felicia on the front steps of the school. "Hey, good luck at the mall," she said. "I hope you get your Shauna shirts."

"We will," I said triumphantly. I could tell she really wanted to come along, so I added, "I'll e-mail you all about it later, 'kay?"

Felicia nodded and smiled. "Okay. I can't wait to see what they look like."

The bus was just pulling up as we sprinted to the stop.

"I am so psyched about our shirts," I said, sliding over in my seat to make room for Amanda. Through the window I watched the school get smaller and smaller in the distance. This was great—just Amanda and me. I really liked hanging out with Felicia and Traci, too, but I missed having Amanda all to myself.

"I'm psyched, too," Amanda said. "Hey, there are these really great shoes at Babe's. Maybe we can head over there after the Shauna thing."

"Yeah, sure," I said. I hoped we'd have time. I had to get back to the school by five-thirty. That's when my dad would be there to pick me up from "soccer practice."

"Is something wrong?" Amanda asked me. I guess I looked tense.

"Just a little bus sick. Hey, that's really pretty." I pointed to a drawing Amanda had taped to the outside of her math book. Amanda's a really talented artist.

"Thanks. Don't you love art class with Mr. Tate? I can't wait till we do mobiles. They're so cool!" Amanda is passionate about everything, especially art class. Mr. Tate had already made a big deal about one of her drawings and put it up on the bulletin board outside the art room. I could barely use a glue stick.

I nodded. "But what about Mr. Reid's math class?" I said.

"Ugh. Don't remind me," Amanda said, rolling her eyes.

"I just hope I can do better in English," I said, popping a piece of gum in my mouth. I offered some to Amanda.

"Mrs. Scott's pretty tough," Amanda agreed, shaking her head at the gum. "She doesn't let you slide on anything."

"Don't I know it," I said, chewing on my grape bubble gum. Real sugar, yum. "I got a C-minus on my last quiz. I've never gotten a C-minus before in my life. And why does she have to give us a quiz every single week? My parents will probably want to send me to about fourteen tutors. It's grammar. I just can't do it."

"Sure you can," Amanda said, ever the cheerleader. "You just need to find a way to make the rules stick in your head."

"Whatever," I said. "I don't even know why I need to learn that stuff if I'm going to be a huge soccer star when I grow up. I mean, I know I'm not going to be an English teacher."

A couple of girls got on the bus. They were wearing gray uniforms like the ones I used to wear at my old school. The girls looked like eighth graders. They bounced down the aisle, chattering away about the Shauna giveaway. I had butterflies the size of elephants in my stomach. I couldn't wait to get my hands on one of those T-shirts.

I whispered to Amanda, "When the doors open, let's go for it."

She nodded, and we stood up and parked ourselves near the back doors of the bus.

The bus pulled up to the mall parking lot. It was crawling with Shauna Ferris fans. I'd wanted to just walk in, all cool, and step right up to the doors of the music store. Now I could see that we were going to have to make a run for it, even if we looked like total idiots doing it.

The doors hissed open. "Run for the doors near the electronics store," I shouted to Amanda, leaping off the last step of the bus into the parking lot. "They're closer to the music store."

What would happen if we weren't one of the first twenty-five people? I couldn't even think about it. Failure was not an option. Amanda and I pushed through the doors. There were only about ten people standing in front of the closed doors of Music Connection, but I could see a ton of girls in Shauna tees heading our way at the other end of the mall by the main entrance. If no one was going to start a line, then it was up to Amanda and me to make one. I camped right in front of the doors, with my feet wide and my elbows out, hands on my hips. Amanda took the same pose behind me. No one was edging past us.

"I guess we're first and second, Amanda," I said loudly.

A cute girl in a white jean skirt and a purple Shauna concert tee stomped up and took her place behind Amanda.

"First come, first served," I said sweetly.

Amanda nudged me. "Arielle, don't be mean."

"Well, I'm third," White Jeans Girl announced. Like I cared.

"Whatever," I said, rolling my eyes. Behind the locked doors of the Music Connection a manager was stacking T-shirts. They were pink—one of my favorite colors.

"This is so cool," I said to Amanda. We were so excited that we actually hugged. I know it sounds a little corny, but it felt like we were part of something really big. Tomorrow we'd be the queens of style with our limited-edition, signed T-shirts. I couldn't wipe the big grin off my face. Not until Miss I'm the

Biggest Shauna Fan started running her mouth off behind us.

"Yeah, I know all the songs by heart. Every single one. My older brother even bought me an import single of 'Angel Boy' that they only sell in England."

Import single? Puh-leeze. Was it just me, or was she really irritating? And anyway, *I* was the biggest Shauna Ferris fan. But the most annoying thing was that the girls around her seemed totally impressed.

The girl kept on bragging. "I can do all the dance moves on the video. You know when she does that thing where she knocks the chair over and does this?" She moved her arm across her face from left to right and rocked in place.

Okay, so she could dance. Big deal. Maybe I shouldn't have let it get to me, but I couldn't help it. Before I knew it, I was off and blabbing.

"Amanda, did I tell you that my mom actually knows Shauna's lawyer?" I said it loud enough for the first ten people in line to hear. Amanda flashed me a warning look. "No, really. It's true. She went to law school with him. So I could meet Shauna anytime I want." It was true. My mom did go to school with Shauna's lawyer. Not that it was doing me any good. My mom wouldn't know Shauna Ferris from the school cafeteria lady. And she hadn't exactly spoken to the guy in about ten years. But she did know him. It wasn't a total lie.

"Yeah, sure," Amanda said. I knew what she meant was, *Who cares? Why are you bragging like that?*

I didn't have much time to respond because the store manager came out and stood in front of the doors with his arms crossed. Some fourth-grade girls in the back started screaming, and I was majorly embarrassed. It wasn't like this guy was Shauna or anything. But what can you expect from fourth graders?

"Okay, Shauna fans," the manager said. "The doors will be open in two minutes. As you know, you'll be the first people to hear Shauna Ferris's new CD. And the first twenty-five people will get signed T-shirts. No pushing. No shoving. And please, no screaming." The line went quiet. We were all dying to get inside.

I swear I could actually hear my heart pounding. More than anything in the world, I wanted Amanda and me to be the first ones to walk out of that store wearing our new T-shirts. The doors opened, and I practically pulled Amanda's arm out of her body.

"Ow. Calm down, okay?" she whined.

"Sorry," I said. I gave the store manager my best smile. "Hi. I'm Arielle, and this is Amanda. May we have two T-shirts, please?"

"Here you go," he said, handing two bright pink shirts to us. I held it up to me and looked at it. There was a picture of Shauna on it, the one they used on her new CD. And in the right-hand corner was her name, Shauna, in her very own handwriting. It was perfect.

"Let's put them on!" I squealed. I pulled mine over my head and stuck my arms through. It was a little big. Okay, so it hung down almost to my knees, but it was mine, all mine.

Amanda didn't seem to be sharing the moment, though. "What's up?" I asked.

"I can't believe you told that girl your mom knows Shauna's lawyer."

"Well, she does. I mean, they're not best buds, but . . ." Suddenly I felt kind of stupid. Amanda was my best friend, wasn't she? Why wasn't she on my side about this? "Look, I just wanted to shut her up. She was all, 'Oh, I'm Shauna's biggest fan. Watch me, I can do her dance moves.'" I moved my hand across my face and spun around like an idiot. Amanda started to laugh, then she got her thoughtful look.

"Seriously, though, Arielle. Why do you have to compete with a total stranger? Who cares if she's Shauna's best friend or has a million import singles?"

Who cares? Me. I wasn't going to let some obnoxious girl get away with that. "Come on. You thought she was annoying, too. Admit it," I said.

We'd wandered over to Bagatelle, my favorite accessories store. A pair of rhinestone butterfly clips caught my eye. Amanda was checking out a tie-dyed scarf. "I guess it just bothers me that you have to prove you're better than everybody else." She shrugged. "Why not just be yourself?"

What did she mean by that? Did my best friend think I was a phony? "I *am* being myself," I snapped.

For a few seconds neither one of us said a word. Then Amanda said, "It's just that you don't always have to be the best, you know."

My face felt red-hot. "What's wrong with trying to be the best?" I asked.

"I'm not trying to hurt your feelings. I'm sorry," Amanda said. I so did not want her to feel sorry for me. And I didn't want to wreck the mood.

"Forget it," I said, putting the clips back on the rack. "Look, maybe I'm not a saint. But I did get you a Shauna T-shirt, right?"

"Totally!" Amanda exclaimed.

She high-fived me, and we looked around to see if anybody was watching. It was sort of a lame thing to do.

"Hey, are you thirsty?" I asked.

"Mm-hmm," Amanda answered. "Let's grab a soda."

"Okay," I said. "And then I want to go to the Sports Palace. There's a soccer jersey I've been wanting for ages."

We ordered two Cokes from the corn dog stand and a side of fries. Standing at the front of a line of frantic Shauna fans had given us an appetite.

"Oh, wait!" Amanda dug a dollar out of her purse and stuffed it into a Feed the Children can by the cash register.

The white-haired woman behind the counter winked at Amanda. "Bless you, honey," she said. She looked at me and waited.

"Um, just a sec," I said, putting down my tray. "I think I've got some money, too." I reached into my backpack and pulled out the wallet my dad had brought me from Italy one time. Without thinking, I grabbed what I thought was a dollar bill. Only when I had it halfway in the can did I realize that it was really a five-dollar bill. Oops. I couldn't exactly pull it back out. That would be so rude. With a sigh I let it drop into the can. There went my new soccer jersey.

"How wonderful! What a good girl," the white-haired lady said, patting my hand. Usually I'd roll my eyes at something like that, but it actually made me feel kind of special.

Amanda got all sappy the way she does around dogs or little kids. "That was the best, Arielle. You can't fool me. I know you're a nice person."

I was glad I'd done it, too. Even if it was kind of a mistake and it meant that the soccer jersey I wanted would have to wait until another time.

"You better eat some of these fries, or I'm going to finish them," Amanda warned.

"Hey, leave some for me!" I reached in, grabbed a handful, and stuck them all in my mouth at once.

We polished off our fries and sodas in record time.

"Come on," Amanda said, tossing our empty

french fry containers in a metal trash can marked Paper. Amanda made sure to recycle everything. "Let's go shopping."

We coasted into Babe's, the coolest clothes store in the universe. Or at least the coolest clothes store in the Wonder Lake Mall.

"Aren't those shoes the best?" I said, pointing to a pair of strappy ice-blue sandals with tiny plastic flowers on the straps.

"Check out the price tag." Amanda made a whistling noise.

"Whoa," I said.

A salesgirl wearing lots of makeup came and stood over us. "Can I help you girls with something?" She was smiling, but her voice had a snotty edge to it. That really bugged me. Just because we were in sixth grade didn't mean we couldn't shop there.

"Uh . . . ," Amanda said, stepping back from the shoes.

I flipped my hair over my shoulders and glanced around the store. "No, thanks. You don't have anything nice enough for us. Come on, Tiffany," I said to Amanda. "Let's go."

Amanda caught on and looped her arm through mine. We put our noses in the air and walked out, stopping by the big fountain. Then we laughed so hard, we nearly fell over.

"She was such a snob," Amanda said, giggling.

"Totally," I said.

Amanda looked at her watch. "Hey, what time did you say your dad was picking us up?" she asked.

My dad! I was having such a good time shopping, I'd totally forgotten we had to be back at school to meet my dad at five-thirty.

"What time is it?" I asked.

Amanda checked her watch. "Five o'clock."

I couldn't believe I'd messed up so badly. It was so not like me. But I'd never done anything like this before—skipping practice, lying to my parents, my coach, and my best friend.

I wasn't as good at it as I thought.

"We have to go!" I squealed, tugging on Amanda's arm and running for the mall exit. "We're going to be late!"

chapter
THREE

E-mail from sockrgrl0 to PrincessA

Hi, Arielle!

How was the CD party? I hope you and Amanda got your T-shirts. Practice was really tough today. Coach Talbot is prepping us for the big game against the Tigers, and we covered a ton of new stuff. Call me and I'll fill you in. Later.

—Traci

"I thought your dad would just pick us up here," Amanda huffed as we ran through the mall parking lot.

"Uh, no, he, ah, he couldn't," I stammered. "He had a meeting near the school and . . . and . . . it was just easier." I didn't know if Amanda bought it or not. We got to the stop just as the bus pulled away.

"Oh, no!" I wailed.

"No big deal." Amanda shrugged. "We'll just catch the next one. It should be here in ten minutes."

Ten minutes! It might as well have been ten hours.

It was at least a fifteen-minute ride back to the school. We'd get there too late. I pictured my frantic dad getting the lowdown from Coach Talbot that I'd skipped practice. There'd be police dogs, a search, news teams. And I'd have to change my identity and move to another state to avoid being grounded till I was thirty.

"Look, here's another one." Amanda pointed down the road. Another blue-and-white city bus pulled up. We hopped on and were home free. Whew.

My dad's black BMW was just driving up to the soccer field when we got off the bus. A new thought hit me: How were we going to get to my dad's car without running into Coach Talbot and the rest of the team? I was in a total panic.

"Let's go this way," I said, walking all the way around the front of the school.

Amanda stopped and looked toward the soccer fields out back. "It's quicker that way."

I kept walking. "Too crowded. I don't want anyone to see our shirts until tomorrow." Did that sound believable?

When we got near the gym, I took my Shauna shirt off and stuffed it into my backpack.

"There's no one around. Why are you doing that?" Amanda asked. I pretended I didn't hear her and made a run for Dad's car.

"Hi, Dad! Can we give Amanda a ride home?" I said breathlessly.

"Sure, honey."

"How was work today?" I chirped. If I could get my dad talking, Amanda wouldn't have time to ask me any more questions.

"Your old man knocked 'em dead, Arielle." Through the back window I could see Coach and the girls coming off the field. We'd just missed them. Finally I could relax. Or so I thought.

"So, Amanda," Dad said. "Are you thinking of trying out for the soccer team? Is that why you went to practice with Miss Hotshot here?"

Usually my dad never even asked *me* about soccer! I couldn't believe he was asking *Amanda*. Why today? What could I do? Would Amanda cover for me? Or was I about to be grounded for life? Slowly it dawned on Amanda what was going on. She turned and glared at me.

I whispered, "Please, please, please."

"Well, no, I, ah, I, um, I just wanted to, you know, support the team since it was their first practice and everything." Amanda's voice was shaky. I knew she was really mad at me. But at least she hadn't blown my cover. Yet.

"That's great. That's what being a good friend is all about," Dad said.

"Yes, I guess so," Amanda said. She practically spit it at me.

Dad wouldn't let it go. "So tell me about practice. What did you do today, Arielle?"

"The usual," I said, trying to get off the subject. "Boring passing drills and stuff."

"That's not a very positive attitude, Arielle. Amanda, you were there. I bet it was a lot more interesting than that."

Oh, no. Dad was putting on his lawyer self. He'd be interrogating Amanda in a minute.

"Well, I don't know much about soccer. But yeah, it was interesting, I guess."

"You see, there," Dad said. He pulled onto Amanda's street. "Amanda thought it was interesting. Glass half full. Glass half empty. It's all about how you see it, Arielle."

"You're so right, Dad," I said with all the enthusiasm I could muster. I could see Amanda's big white house coming up on our right. "We're here, Dad," I said, pointing it out.

Dad laughed. "I think I know where Amanda lives."

"Right," I said. I was blabbering like an idiot. Or a guilty person.

"Thanks for the ride, Mr. Davis," Amanda said, and hopped out of the car. I waited for her to say good-bye to me, but she just slammed the door and walked up the hill to her house without a word.

"Dad, can you wait a sec?"

I ran after her. "Amanda, wait up!" Amanda turned around and crossed her arms, waiting for an apology. Gulp. I guess I owed her one. "I'm sorry. It's just that

I didn't think you'd go if I told you I was skipping practice."

"So you lied to me."

"I didn't lie, I just—"

"Arielle, you did. You lied to me. Your best friend. And then I had to cover for you with your dad. So now I've lied, too."

I hadn't thought about it that way before. Lies sure had a way of growing. Still, we'd had fun. I put my hands on my hips and looked her right in the face. "Are you sorry you went?"

Amanda let out a little growl. She does that when she's frustrated. "That's not the point. What are you going to tell Coach Talbot and the team tomorrow?"

"So I skipped a practice. It's no big deal. I'm the best player on the team," I said.

"And the team needs you. When you're not there, they have to play around you," Amanda insisted.

I said the first thing that popped into my head. "If they can't play right, that's their problem—not mine."

Amanda's mouth opened, then closed. "That is so selfish, Arielle Davis."

Selfish? She called me *selfish*? And she used my last name, just like my mom does when she's mad at me. So uncool. Who did Amanda think she was, anyway?

"Well, if I'm so selfish, maybe you should just give me back that Shauna T-shirt I got for you."

"You got for me? I got it myself!"

"You wouldn't have gone if I hadn't helped you," I said.

"Never mind. I'm going inside," Amanda said, turning to go.

"Whatever," I said, and marched off to the car.

From the backseat I could see Amanda closing the big red door to her house. I wondered if I'd ever see the inside of that house again.

"You two looked like you were fighting." Dad peered at me in the rearview mirror.

"It's nothing," I muttered. Thankfully, Dad let it go.

Selfish? I was not selfish.

Our housekeeper, Anya, greeted me as I breezed through the front door, hurling my backpack onto the sofa.

Anya stopped vacuuming, took one look at me, and knew something wasn't right. "You have a bad day, Arielle?" she asked in her thick Russian accent. Anya had worked for my family for four years, and she was really sweet. I didn't want her to worry about me, so I added one more lie to my daily total.

"No. It was a really good day, Anya," I said, trying to smile.

"I put cookies in the kitchen," Anya said, smiling at me. "That will make you happy."

"Okay," I said. She went back to vacuuming.

I checked our answering machine. There was a call from the dentist, one from the rug cleaners, and one from somebody collecting coats for the Salvation Army. No call from Amanda or Traci or Felicia.

Selfish.

I wasn't selfish.

I trudged upstairs and flopped on my bed. I loved my white-lace canopy bed. It always made me feel safe and relaxed. From my desk in the corner my computer stared at me. I went over and logged on. Traci had sent me an e-mail marked Urgent. She probably wanted me to work at the animal shelter. I really couldn't deal with that now. Instead I opened an e-mail from Felicia.

To: PrincessA
From: FiFio1

Hi, Arielle.

How's it going? Did you and Amanda get the shirts? Was it amazing? You've got to tell me everything.

Love,

Felicia

P.S. Decorating birthday cakes is a lot harder than it looks on TV.

At least Felicia was still my friend. I fired back a reply.

To: FiFiol
From: PrincessA

Hey, Felicia.
  Yes, it was wild. Lots of girls were there. But we made our way to the front of the line. The shirts are so cool! They're pink with a picture of Shauna and her signature down in the corner.

I was thinking about Amanda calling me selfish, so I added a P.S.

I'll let you borrow it sometime.

Felicia must have still been on her computer because in a few minutes she sent me an instant message.

FiFiol: That is so great about the shirts! You are really sweet to let me wear it.

Sweet. She'd called me sweet, not selfish. So there.

I'm glad you think so, I wrote back. *Amanda's pretty mad at me.*
Felicia responded. *Why?*
Should I tell Felicia what really happened? I was

sure when she heard my side of things, she'd understand that Amanda was getting mad over nothing. So I zapped back the whole story.

I waited for Felicia to write back, but she didn't. Instead the phone rang.

"Hello?" I said, hoping to hear Amanda's voice on the other end. It was Felicia.

"Oh, my gosh," she said. "No wonder she's so mad at you."

Oh, no. Felicia didn't understand, either. "She shouldn't be mad at me," I said sulkily. "After all, if it hadn't been for me, she wouldn't have a Shauna T-shirt now."

Felicia was quiet for a few seconds. I could hear her breathing on the other end. "Well, you did kind of put her in a bad position, Arielle. She had to lie for you."

Lying? It wasn't really lying. It was just . . . fibbing. A little bit. Why was everyone making such a big deal about this? "I thought you were my friend," I accused.

"I am your friend," she said. "But what you did was wrong. Sorry, but that's how I feel. Please don't be mad at me."

But I was mad at her. I thought she'd be on my side.

"I better go. I'll talk to you later," I said gloomily.

It got quiet again on Felicia's end. Then she said softly, "Sure. See you at school."

And then she hung up first. I was the one who was mad, and she hung up first. This day was turning out to be a serious disaster. I needed to cheer myself up, *fast*.

When Dad was safely in his study and Anya was busy making dinner before Mom got home, I sneaked down the stairs and grabbed my backpack. In my room I pulled out the pink Shauna T-shirt and pulled it over my head. It was definitely cool. And only twenty-five of us had them in the whole town. I wondered if Amanda would wear hers to school tomorrow or skip it out of protest over what I'd done.

In the mirror my reflection stared back at me. At my straight auburn hair with the cowlick. At my small mouth and creamy skin. At my determined green eyes. It didn't seem like a selfish face to me. Tomorrow I would make everything right. I'd work extra hard in school and on the soccer field. I'd be good to my parents and load up the dishwasher. I'd fix things.

And if Amanda and Felicia couldn't see that I needed to skip practice to get a Shauna T-shirt, well, maybe Traci would understand. I might not have three best friends anymore, but at least I had one. Sort of. Maybe.

chapter
FOUR

Ms. McClintic's Questionnaire

Q: If you could change anything about yourself, what would it be?

A: If there was something to change, I would have done it already. So I guess I wouldn't change anything.

Does this make me sound totally conceited? I hate this assignment.

"Hey, great shirt," a seventh-grade girl said while we were standing in the lunch line.

"Thanks," I replied quietly.

I loved the shirt, but I kind of wished I hadn't worn it after all. It was like a walking reminder of everything that had gone wrong in the past twenty-four hours.

I filled up my tray and headed over to our usual table. Most days lunch is my favorite period. But today the walk from the lunch line to the table where Amanda, Felicia, and Traci were already sitting felt like the longest walk of my life. Traci and Felicia had had an orchestra dress rehearsal that morning, and they were both wearing their nerdy black-and-white concert outfits. Amanda hadn't talked to me all day. She was wearing a Save Our Forests shirt instead of her Shauna T-shirt.

"Hi," I said, trying to sound extra cheery as I plunked my plastic tray down next to Felicia. "Is this tuna casserole gross or what?"

Amanda and Felicia didn't even smile. Traci shrugged. They were definitely giving me the cold shoulder.

Amanda stood up. "I'll catch you all later. I've got to study for my vocab quiz. Bye." She didn't even look at me. She just turned and dumped her tray and left.

Traci and Felicia were watching me, waiting for me to say something. I cocked my head like I didn't care.

"Whatever," I said.

Felicia took a sip of her apple juice. "Yeah, she's still pretty mad at you." Her tone said, *And I am, too.*

I was starting to feel like the face on a wanted poster. I turned my back to Felicia and smiled at Traci. She had a really cute butterfly clip in her hair. "I like that clip. Did you get it at Bagatelle?" I asked, hoping to win her over.

Traci dropped her fork onto her plate. "Arielle, don't you think you should apologize to Amanda? You really put her on the spot yesterday."

Okay, so the butterfly clip compliment hadn't worked. But did she have to butt into my fight with Amanda? It was none of her business.

"Sorry that you have to eat lunch with such a known criminal," I said sarcastically.

Traci's eyes narrowed. "You can be so impossible sometimes, Arielle."

"It's my best quality," I said, trying to keep my voice unconcerned. "Besides, this is between me and Amanda. It doesn't have anything to do with you."

Traci came back at me. "It does so have to do with me! I had to play center forward for you yesterday. The whole team had to play without you."

She sounded just like Amanda.

Felicia put down her juice box. "Maybe we should just drop it for now." She looked from Traci to me hopefully. Felicia hates it when we fight.

I took a bite of my casserole.

I wanted to know more about yesterday's practice, but I didn't want Traci to think I was worried. "So," I said between bites of noodles, "how did practice go? You just did a lot of basic drills and stuff, right?"

Traci shook her head. "Didn't you get my e-mail?"

E-mail? I flashed back to last night, my computer, the unread message. Oops. "Uh—uh . . ." I stammered.

Traci sighed. "I gave you the lowdown on soccer practice. We covered a lot of new moves. Some team plays I'd never seen before. It was pretty tricky stuff."

I was starting to get a little nervous. "What kinds of moves?"

"There was this thing Coach Talbot showed us

where we pass to the center forward, pass back, and pass outside," Traci explained.

"Doesn't sound too tough," I said. I couldn't believe I was freaking out over something so silly. Just because Traci the klutz couldn't handle it didn't mean I couldn't.

"Arielle, this was really advanced. They didn't even cover it in AYSO." Was it my imagination, or was Traci trying to scare me?

"Well, maybe they didn't cover it in little old South Carolina soccer, but at Country Day Soccer Camp we covered everything," I huffed.

"Fine," Traci said, standing up. "You know, Arielle, I was trying to help you. But you can be such a snob sometimes. And now you've started lying, too. I'm not sure I want to be friends with somebody I can't trust." She glared at me. The kids at the next table were watching. It was so embarrassing.

"Oh, yeah? Well, at least I don't look like a penguin," I said. The kids at the next table snickered.

I looked over at Felicia, but she had her head down. Of course, she was wearing the same outfit as Traci. Oops. I knew I should apologize, but I couldn't seem to make the words *I'm sorry* come out of my mouth.

Traci's face was beet red. "Fine. I just thought you should know about the new stuff." She turned to go.

"Wait for me," Felicia said, hurrying after her.

I was alone at the table. Just me and my big mouth.

The rest of the day was torture. The clock actually seemed to be moving backward. In English, I pretended to read over my chapter on conjunctions like everybody else. But my book might have been upside down for all I got out of it. And my three so-called best friends hadn't said a word to me since lunch.

I wondered what it was going to be like out on the soccer field. I pictured myself standing in the middle of the field, being trampled by eight girls who were using Coach Talbot's fancy new plays.

Bad attitude, I scolded myself. I had to psych myself up to play well. I tried to picture myself using the new drills like I'd known them my whole life. I was running down the field. The goal was right in front of me. I kicked and scored.

The bell rang, and I breezed past Traci, Amanda, and Felicia on my way to the gym. I didn't even stop to put my books away. I wanted a few minutes to stretch and warm up by myself.

The soccer field was pretty muddy from the rain we'd had that morning. I hated playing in the mud, but I couldn't let that throw me.

I bent over to retie my shoe on the bench. Sarah Johnson came up and clapped me on the back. She was an eighth grader and the team's captain. Next to me, she was the best player on the team. "We missed you yesterday. Where were you?"

I didn't know what to say. "Didn't Coach Talbot tell you?"

Sarah rolled her eyes. "You know Coach Talbot. She only talks about the game."

I fumbled for an answer. Should I tell Sarah the truth, or should I stick with my story about being sick? I decided to change the subject. "I heard you learned some new moves yesterday."

Sarah nodded, and her long brown ponytail bobbed up and down. "Just wait'll you see the new plays. They're really hard but so cool!"

Even Sarah thought the new stuff was hard? Now I was nervous again. Out of the corner of my eye I saw Traci sitting on a bench, tying her shoes. I hoped she wouldn't tell Coach Talbot why I'd really been out. Suddenly I just wanted practice to be over.

Coach Talbot called roll. When she got to my name, she stopped and looked at me. "Feeling better, Arielle?"

My face got really hot. I started to sweat. I could feel Traci waiting for me to confess everything. "Uh, yes, Coach. I'm ready to play."

"Glad to hear it," Coach Talbot said. Whew. I was safe. Coach Talbot continued. "Okay, I'll give a brief recap of yesterday's moves. Arielle, just try to keep up. If you need help, look to Sarah and Jenny here. Here we go. Red team on the right, white team on the left."

I didn't need any help. I was going to show Coach Talbot and everyone else that I could miss a practice and still play better than ever. I was going to take the white team to victory, no matter what.

Coach Talbot blew her whistle, and Sarah threw in the first ball. I was ready to play hard, but I couldn't even get near the action. A red team player swiped the ball right out from under me and passed it off so fast, I didn't know what had happened. It took me five whole seconds to realize they were all at the other end of the field. I ran hard to catch up and got there just as the red team scored a goal. It was them, one; us, zero. Zero is so not my favorite number.

Coach blew her whistle and called out to me. "Arielle! You okay? You're looking a little lost out there."

There was no way I was letting Coach Talbot take me off the field and replace me with Traci. Like Traci needed one more reason to say, *I told you so.* My whole soccer career at Wonder Lake depended on getting the new plays down, pronto.

After a few minutes of getting pushed, shoved, knocked over, and left behind, I was covered in mud and watching the red team score another goal. That was it. This time I was going for it.

"Sarah," I huffed. "Pass me the ball this time."

"Didn't I tell you this was tricky stuff?" she said, grinning.

The whistle blew, and Sarah headed the ball right to me. I moved down the muddy field like wildfire. I could hear Sarah screaming at me to pass to her, but there was no way I was giving up the ball till I kicked it right past the goalie and into the net. The next minute was a blur. A red team girl jumped in front of me. My whole body got confused. I went to kick, and so did she, and then I was falling, an awful, hot pain searing my right calf as I fell down in the mud.

"Ow!" I screamed, grabbing my leg. It hurt so much.

Coach Talbot raced over. Her eyebrows were knitted together in concern. "Can you walk, Arielle?"

I stood up and nearly crumpled. Coach put her arm around me, and we hopped off the field. "Traci McClintic. I need you to sub for Davis here."

"Sure, Coach," Traci said. Behind Coach Talbot's back she shook her head at me and then ran onto the field to play center forward. My position.

Coach Talbot stretched out my leg and put an ice bag on it. My leg throbbed from the pain and the cold. I watched as Traci did the play perfectly and scored a goal for white. Now my pride was aching, too.

I handed the ice bag back to Coach Talbot. "It's okay. Just give me a minute. I can still play."

She put the ice bag right back on. "Let's see what the doctor has to say about that, okay?"

Doctor? An equation filled my head: Doctor equals parents equals trouble. I groaned.

"Are you all right, Arielle?" the coach asked me.

I looked at my mud-splattered cleats. I'd be in even deeper mud soon. "I'm fine," I whispered. "Just great."

chapter
FIVE

Arielle's Shopping List on the Fridge

Scrunchies—not plaid or the kinds with pom-poms on
  the end
Cool teen magazine
Double Dutch chocolate ice cream
Ace bandage
New leg

"Tell me it's not broken," Mom said dramatically when she entered the emergency room. She was still dressed in her navy blue suit. I hoped she hadn't been in the middle of a trial or something.

Dad was right behind her, wearing his favorite gray pin-striped suit. He looked worried. I wanted to remember them like this—worried about me and *nice*. Once they heard the whole truth, they'd look a lot different.

The doctor beamed at my mother. "Mrs. Davis, she's going to be fine. It's just a pulled muscle."

"How did it happen?" Mom asked.

Uh-oh.

Coach Talbot stood next to my bed with her hands on her hips. "Arielle was playing a little recklessly. She went in for an aggressive play and took a big slide."

Dad's face went cloudy. "That doesn't sound like our Arielle. She never misses a shot."

"She's a great little competitor, that's true," Coach Talbot agreed. "If she hadn't been out sick yesterday and missed such a crucial practice, she would have been up on our new plays."

I wanted to crawl into a hole and disappear.

"I don't understand," Mom said, raising her chin and looking down her nose at Coach Talbot the way she does when she's cross-examining a witness. "Arielle wasn't sick yesterday. She told us she went to practice."

"Mom . . ."

Dad put his arm around Mom. "I picked her up myself at five-thirty by the soccer fields."

"Dad . . ."

Coach Talbot crossed her arms and gave me a long, hard look. "Well, I'm sorry to tell you that she wasn't at practice yesterday. Maybe Arielle can tell us where she was."

Three pairs of accusing eyes shifted my way. "Mom, Dad, Coach Talbot, I can explain everything. . . ."

And I did. Or I tried to. The more I talked, the worse it got.

"We'll discuss this when we get home," Mom announced briskly. Translated, that meant, *You are serious toast, young lady*.

Coach Talbot shook her head and leveled her blue eyes at me. "I have to say I'm really disappointed in you, Arielle. You've got a lot of talent, but it takes more than talent to be part of a winning team. Lying and skipping practices isn't something I tolerate in my players."

A lump rose in my throat. "Yes, ma'am," I whispered.

"I expect to see an improvement in your attitude, Arielle. Do you understand?" she asked.

I nodded. I felt like I was going to cry. I stared down at my leg. My stupid, stupid leg.

Dad signed my release papers. The doctor wrapped my leg in an Ace bandage and told me I'd be coming back for physical therapy twice a week for the next two weeks.

"How will I fit that in with soccer practice?" I asked, wincing a little as I hopped off the bed.

He laughed and helped me into a wheelchair. "Sorry, kid. You're officially benched till your leg's better."

"You can cheer the team on from the sidelines," Coach Talbot said.

But I was center forward. Or I had been. I couldn't stand the thought that Traci would be out there playing my position while I sat on the sidelines and watched.

"B-but the team needs me!" I wailed. "We've got our first game in two weeks!"

Dad furrowed his bristly eyebrows at me. "We can talk about how you let the team down when we get home."

Mom pulled the car up to the front entrance of the hospital, and Dad helped me into the backseat.

As we drove away, I watched the hospital through the back window. From the top of the hill it looked like a prison. My prison, for the next two weeks.

At home Mom and Dad sat me on the couch while they took turns pacing and talking. It was what they did in court all day long. I guess it's kind of hard to turn it off. After a lot of "how could you do this" from them and "I'm sorry" from me, they handed down their sentence: no more Shauna Ferris. They were taking away my CDs, my posters, the TV in my room, even my brand-new T-shirt.

"Let the punishment fit the crime," Dad announced, crossing his arms.

"For how long?" I squeaked.

Mom grabbed my new teen mag with Shauna on the cover and rolled it up. "Until you can prove that you can behave responsibly and earn our trust again."

My parents had never been able to ground me for longer than half a day. They always caved in.

I hung my head in shame and looked up at them with big eyes. Nothing. Nada. They were like stone statues. Gulp. "Mom, Dad, I know I made a mistake, but I promise I'll never do it again. Just give me another chance." Time to go for the kill. "Please?"

"That's not going to work this time, young lady. That was a very serious offense you committed."

I couldn't believe it. It was so not fair. It's not like I'd run wild in the streets or anything. I'd just skipped one lousy soccer practice. Why was I being punished as if I'd robbed a bank?

The doorbell rang. I grabbed my crutches and hobbled over, thankful for the interruption. When I opened the door, Amanda was standing there.

"Hi," she said. It wasn't a normal "hi," but at least she was talking to me.

"Hi," I said. "Want to come in?"

We sat on the couch. "I brought you your books. I heard about your leg from Traci. Bummer."

"Yeah," I said. "Guess I won't be doing any shoe shopping anytime soon."

She gave me sort of a half smile. "So, do your parents know that you skipped practice?"

"Yup." I sighed. "They know everything. They've gone off the deep end about it. No Shauna Ferris till I'm eighteen, I guess."

Amanda made a whistling noise. "Wow. Sorry twice. Maybe they'll change their minds."

"No way. I'm lucky I'm not doing hard labor." I sighed again.

Amanda pointed to my Ace bandage. "But you're an invalid."

"Good point," I said, smiling. It was starting to feel like we were friends again.

"So," Amanda said quietly. "When can you play soccer again?"

"That's the worst part." I groaned. "I have to sit out for two whole weeks and go to physical therapy twice a week at the hospital."

"Traci said her brother, Dave, had to do physical therapy for a skateboard injury. It really helped."

Traci's older brother was an eighth grader at Wonder Lake. I knew Amanda kind of had a crush on him.

"I don't think it'll take two weeks to heal," I said confidently. "I'll be back playing soccer in a week, tops."

"Arielle . . ." Amanda gave me a warning look.

"I mean, look," I said, standing up. "I can put some weight on it."

I took a step. Hot pain raced up my leg and sent me crashing to the floor. "Ouch!"

"Are you okay?" Amanda put her arm around me and helped me to the couch. "No offense, but that was a really silly thing to do, Arielle."

My leg throbbed. Upstairs, my parents had locked up my favorite hobby. And I couldn't even walk. Not counting yesterday, this had been the worst day of my life.

"Why is this happening to me?" I moaned.

Amanda shrugged. "Well, you did skip practice. . . ."

I couldn't believe Amanda didn't feel even slightly sorry for me. "Oh, right. It's all my fault. Thanks for reminding me."

"Arielle, I didn't mean anything. . . ."

I picked up my grammar book. "Sorry to make you come over for nothing," I said hollowly. "See you tomorrow."

Amanda crossed her arms and sighed loudly. "You could at least say thanks for bringing your books."

"Thanks," I said without looking up.

That's all it took to make Amanda snap.

"Hurting your leg didn't teach you anything," she cried. "You're still acting totally selfish. I'll see you tomorrow."

Then she stomped out of the living room and closed the door just a little harder than usual.

I couldn't get over what she'd said. Twice.

Selfish. Me?

chapter
six

Contents of Arielle's Backpack

English textbook (even if it never comes out of the
    bag, some grammar rules might get memorized
    via osmosis)
New one-of-a-kind Shauna Ferris T-shirt (Mom's not
    getting her hands on this)
Peaches and Cream lip gloss (never leave home
    without it)
Hairbrush (ditto)
Extra-sugary bubble gum (ditto)

"Uh-oh, she's handing back the quizzes," Ryan said.
He put both hands over the sides of his mouth like a
trumpet and started singing "Taps."

Mrs. Scott laughed and placed his essay, facedown,
on his desk. "You can relax, Ryan. Yours was very good."

"Oh, yes!" Ryan said, punching a fist into the air.
"Hey, Gimpy, what did you get?"

I guessed he was talking to me. Most days I would have found that funny. But I wasn't in the mood for jokes today. I rolled my head Ryan's way and fixed him with a glare. "None of your beeswax."

"Oh, she got me." He put his hand over his heart. "Wow, Crutch Girl. I haven't heard that one since first grade. Beeswax. Ooh, I'm scared."

Traci and Amanda were both ignoring me. But Felicia broke down and passed me a note. *How is your leg?* She'd drawn a little frowny face with crutches.

I scribbled a quick answer. *It hurts. Does it look totally stupid?*

Felicia shook her head. Mrs. Scott handed Felicia her quiz. She'd gotten an A-minus. Traci showed Felicia hers with a big red A on the top. They smiled at each other.

Whatever.

I tried not to be nervous. Maybe my quiz would have an A at the top, too. Mrs. Scott dropped it face-down on my desk. I took a deep breath and turned the top corner of it over. A big red C-minus stared back at me. *Not again.* There was a note on the side that said, *See me.* Not a good note to get.

From my desk I could see Amanda's paper with a large A-plus written in red at the top. A-plus as in perfect. Then I noticed that she also had a see-me note. What was up?

Mrs. Scott sat on the edge of her desk. Her heavy black glasses hung from a chain around her neck.

"As you can see, a lot of you had some trouble with your grammar. When you lose a point for each grammar mistake, that can really add up."

I raised my hand. "Mrs. Scott? Why is grammar so important? I mean, it's not like it's going to save my life or anything."

A few kids laughed. Mrs. Scott put on her glasses. "Really?" She wrote a sentence on the board.

Give the medicine to Terry Simon and Bruce.

"Who knows what the meaning of this sentence is?"

"Easy," said Ryan. "You're supposed to give the medicine to this Terry Simon guy and to somebody named Bruce."

Mrs. Scott added a comma between *Terry* and *Simon* and after *Simon*. *Give the medicine to Terry, Simon, and Bruce.* "But what if this is what the doctor really meant? Are we giving the medicine to two people or three? You see what a difference those little commas can make?"

She had a point. But it didn't make me feel better about the C-minus. My parents were going to be even more disappointed in me.

"I was going to move on to poetry this week, but I think we need to spend a little extra time on vocabulary and grammar," Mrs. Scott said.

There were some groans.

Mrs. Scott held up her hands. "All right, that's enough." She was a small woman, but her voice was all business. "You have ten minutes till assembly. I'd like you to spend the rest of the period reviewing chapter two in your grammar books."

I'd forgotten that today was assembly day. At three o'clock we'd all go to our homerooms, where representatives from the different clubs would come and talk to us about joining. There were a lot of different things to belong to—everything from the history club to chess club. The class got noisy as kids started talking about what clubs they wanted to join.

"You may start reading now. Mouths closed. Minds open, please," Mrs. Scott reminded us.

The class settled down. Books flipped open, and pages rustled. With a sigh I ruffled through the pages of my grammar book till I got to chapter two.

"Arielle? Amanda? Could I see you both, please?" Mrs. Scott called from her desk. I guessed it was see-me time. I hoped it wasn't going to be too awful. I was in enough trouble already.

Felicia and Traci gave Amanda worried looks when she passed by. She shrugged. No one looked at me at all. Amanda and I stood in front of Mrs. Scott's desk.

"Arielle, you seem to be having some trouble with the material," Mrs. Scott said. No kidding. She turned to Amanda. "Amanda, you're doing very well."

Could she rub it in a little more?

"I know the two of you are good friends," Mrs. Scott continued. *Were* good friends, I wanted to correct her. "I was thinking that maybe you could tutor Arielle, Amanda. For extra credit."

Was she joking? Me, tutored by Amanda, my former best friend? How could she teach me anything when we weren't even talking to each other?

I started to tell Mrs. Scott it was a bad idea. That I'd just study four times harder. But then Amanda said, "Sure," just like that.

Mrs. Scott smiled. "Great. Then it's settled."

Hello? Did I have any say in this whole setup? We walked back to our seats. For the rest of the class I pretended to look at words on a page in my book, but I couldn't concentrate. I couldn't believe I'd been humiliated like that. Amanda already thought I was selfish. She didn't need another reason to feel superior to me.

Just before the bell rang, Mrs. Hoffman, the school secretary, made an announcement over the loudspeaker.

"Attention, sixth graders. Please report to your homerooms for assembly. Thank you."

The intercom squeaked off, and the bell rang. I stuffed my book in my backpack and slipped my arms through. Ryan surprised me and handed me my crutches. I saw Traci's face fall. I knew she thought he was cute, even though he teased her about her southern accent a lot.

"Thanks," I said. I gave him just a small, polite smile. Even if Traci and I weren't talking, I didn't want her to think I was flirting with her crush.

"No problem," he said. "Peg Leg."

I didn't have time to respond. I wanted to get to my locker without having to thump my way past Felicia, Traci, and Amanda. No such luck. My crutches made it hard for me to get through the aisles easily. I got to the door just as the other girls did.

"Guess we're going to have to talk to each other now," I said coolly to Amanda.

"Guess so," Amanda said.

"Come on, you two," Felicia said, biting her nails. "Let's just all be friends, okay?"

"I'm not the one who doesn't want to be friends," I said.

"Come on," Traci said to Amanda, ignoring me completely. "We better get to homeroom."

Amanda shot me a hurt glare and turned to go.

Felicia backed away. "I better go, too."

I was so mad, I sped down the hall on my crutches and nearly knocked over a guy in jeans and a white shirt who was standing in the doorway of Ms. McClintic's classroom.

"Whoa," he said, backing up.

"Sorry," I muttered. I looked at him for the first time. Brown hair, brown eyes, really cute. There was something familiar about him. Then I recognized him: he was in the auditorium on Monday when I'd hidden from Coach Talbot. I hoped he wouldn't recognize me as the dork who'd asked him where to find the library. I kept my head down and hobbled toward my desk.

"Are you feeling okay, Arielle?" Ms. McClintic said, looking concerned.

"Fine," I whispered, resting my crutches against my desk.

Ms. McClintic called roll and introduced our "guest." The boy in the white shirt was Asher Bank, an eighth grader and president of student government. Ms. McClintic handed out applications for student government to all of us. I noticed she had chalk all over the seat of her pants. Traci noticed it, too.

"Mom," Traci whispered. "Alk-chay on the utt-bay."

"Hmmm? Oh, my goodness, look at me. I'm a mess." Ms. McClintic laughed. Traci slid a little lower in her seat. At least I wasn't the only one being embarrassed today.

Asher smiled at us. On a scale of one to ten, his smile was around a twenty. "Hi," he said. "I'm Asher Bank. I'm going to talk to you about student government today. Student government is a great way to get involved with your school, with other students, with teachers, and even with the town of Wonder Lake. If you've got an idea you want to try, this is the place to try it. And if there's something you don't like, this is the place to get it changed."

A hand went up. Ryan again. "Can we get rid of that dog food spaghetti they've been serving up in the cafeteria every Friday?"

What a dork. But Asher didn't miss a beat. "Sign up and maybe you could run the food committee."

Okay. So Asher was so cute, it was hard not to want to join the student government.

"The meetings are held after school on the last Thursday of the month in the auditorium." He looked right at me. "That's just down the hall from the library. You know, the place where all the books are."

I wanted to crawl under my desk. I doodled on a piece of paper and avoided looking at anyone. A few kids asked questions. Ms. McClintic thanked Asher for coming and told us all what a great opportunity this was to show school spirit. Amanda started filling out her application right away. She'd probably be great at that, too. I stuffed mine in my backpack with my C-minus paper and my useless English book.

"Why don't you sign up, Arielle?" Traci whispered to me. It was the first nice thing she'd said to me. But I was too mad to be nice back.

"I'm already busy playing center forward, remember?" I whispered, glaring at her.

Traci's eyes narrowed. "I'm not trying to take your spot, Arielle. I'm the one who told Coach Talbot to make you center forward in the first place. Remember?" she reminded me.

"Okay, everybody," Ms. McClintic called in a sunny voice. "Now we're going to hear from members of the yearbook staff and the drama club."

After hearing from the pep squad (go, Muskrats!), the history club (boring), and the Latin club (double boring), I was feeling tired and grouchy. I wondered if they had a club for girls with no friends. All I could think about was going home and listening to my Shauna CDs. Then I remembered that I couldn't listen to them anymore because they'd been confiscated. And then I remembered that I had my first physical therapy appointment today. Groan.

When the bell rang, I went to my locker. It was a little hard trying to get my books while balancing on crutches, but I wasn't about to ask for help from any of my so-called friends. A few feet away Amanda and Traci put away their books and chatted about all the different clubs they wanted to join. Felicia came running up to them.

"Oh, my gosh," she said breathlessly. "Did you see that cute guy who's president of student government?"

"Yes." Traci giggled. "Asher Bank. He seems really nice, too."

"I'm definitely applying for student government," Amanda said. "I really want to make a difference this year."

Suddenly it went quiet, and then I could hear them whispering softly. And I thought I heard my name. I couldn't stand it. I slammed my locker door shut and hobbled off to wait for Mom out front.

"Arielle, wait!" Felicia called after me. But I didn't slow down, and I didn't turn around. I just kept going till I was out the door and Mom's Mercedes was in view.

If they wanted to have their own club—the jerks of all time club—fine. They could have it without me.

chapter
SEVEN

List of Magazines at Wonder Lake Hospital

Family Circle
Scientific American
Reptile Quarterly
Business Journal
Golf Digest
Fit After 50
Motherhood
Orthopedic Warehouse

"Are you Arielle Davis?"

A big man with curly black hair and wire-rimmed glasses looked down at a clipboard and then at me.

"Yes," I answered. "That's me."

He smiled and shook my hand. "Hi, Arielle. I'm Mr. Thompson, the physical therapist here at Wonder Lake Hospital. But you can call me Ray. I'm going to help you get that leg back in shape."

I was a little nervous about my first physical therapy appointment. And sitting around in the chilly waiting room at Wonder Lake Hospital hadn't helped. But Ray Thompson put me at ease right away. I hoped he'd fix my leg. I hoped physical therapy wouldn't hurt. But mostly I hoped I wouldn't make a complete idiot of myself. I'd done enough of that lately.

Ray led me into a big room filled with all kinds of exercise equipment. An older woman was sitting on some kind of rowing machine, working on her shoulders. A man with white hair and twinkly eyes sat on some blue mats, trying to touch his toes. He stopped about midknee and groaned. I was the youngest person there by about forty years.

"Very good, Mr. O'Brien. You're making progress." Ray saluted him, and the white-haired man grinned.

"I'm seventy-two, Ray. How much progress can I make?"

"As much as you allow yourself to, my friend," Ray said. "Okay, Arielle. Let's see what you're made of. Hop up."

Ray helped me up onto a padded table and started hooking my calf up to a machine with tons of wires coming out of it. He applied some sticky cold gel to my leg and attached the wires.

"This is electrical stimulation," he said, like he was talking about having peanut butter and jelly for lunch. "It sends little wake-up signals to your muscles and tells them it's time to stop hurting and start healing.

I'm going to adjust the current. You tell me if it's too much."

He turned a knob, and I felt a little tickling sensation like lots of ants on my leg. He kept turning it up till I said stop. I could feel my leg tensing and relaxing, kind of like a massage. It felt kind of good.

Twenty minutes later Ray came back and unhooked me. "Now for the real work."

Now I understood why they call it physical therapy. Ray had me do all sorts of weird exercises. It was mostly a lot of what Ray called "gentle stretching," but it didn't feel gentle. It hurt.

"Ouch," I said, flexing my foot as hard as I could.

"Take it easy," Ray said. "This isn't a contest." I let up a little bit until I felt just a tug with no pain.

"So you're a big soccer star, I hear," Ray said, pointing to my soccer jersey. It was the most comfortable shirt I owned, and I definitely wanted to be comfortable for this.

"Yes, I guess so," I said. "Not right now, though."

"No worries. You'll be streaking down the field again soon. Can you point your toes?" Ray asked, writing some stuff on a chart.

I tried pointing my toes. My leg ached. How could one little strain hurt so badly? "I bet your friends are all pretty upset you've been benched like this, right?" Ray said.

"Sure," I said weakly. I liked Ray. I didn't want him

to think I was a loser who had no friends anymore.

An assistant called Ray to the desk. "I'll be right back," he said. "Don't go away."

I waited and noticed pictures on the wall of Ray with his kids—fishing, swimming, camping. I couldn't remember the last time my whole family had done something together.

Ray walked back into the room. "Hey, Arielle, that was your mom. Her golf game's running over, so she's going to be a little late. You can wait out in the lobby. We've got a soda machine down that first hall to your left. I'll see you on Friday after school."

"Okay. See you Friday," I said.

I hobbled out to the lobby to wait for Mom. I wished I had a magazine to read. The only magazines in the waiting room were all about medicine and other boring stuff.

"Mom, I think we drop the cookies off over here." I recognized that voice. It was Felicia. Up ahead I could see her and her mom. I'd forgotten that they sometimes dropped off cookies from the bakery for the children's ward. I started to call out to Felicia, but then I remembered the way she and Amanda and Traci had been whispering by our lockers after assembly. Forget it. I didn't want to talk to her. I didn't want her to even see me. But where could I hide?

I ducked into the nearest room.

"Can I help you?" In a bed by the windows was a girl about my age with her leg and arm in a cast. Her leg was hanging midair, in traction.

I was so embarrassed about barging into her room, I could barely speak. "I'm sorry. I got lost." I didn't know what to say. "I'm really sorry," I said again.

"It's okay," she said. She noticed my soccer jersey. "Do you play?"

"Uh, yeah. I mean, yes, I play for the Muskrats," I said.

"The state champions," she said. She sounded impressed.

"That's right," I said. "We're the best." It felt good to be on a winning team.

"What position do you play?" she asked.

I loved telling people my position. "Center forward," I said confidently.

"No way! Me too," she said. "I'm Lisa Marconi. I play for the Tigers. Or I did, before I had a major blowout on my bike."

Lisa Marconi. That name seemed familiar. Oh, my gosh. I'd heard about her at camp. She was one of the best soccer players in the state! She was a seventh grader, but she'd done all-state—where they pick the best players from around the state—when she was just a sixth grader. And I'd just acted like a total jerk in front of her.

"Weren't you all-state last year?" I asked, wincing.

"Yeah," she said, like it was no big deal. She had the coolest haircut. It was short and blond with bangs. I'd seen it in a teen magazine and wished I had the nerve to try it. She was wearing some earrings I'd seen at the mall—the same pair of earrings I'd wanted for months. "Hey, my team is playing yours next week."

"Yeah, I know," I said. I was still hoping I'd be playing in that game. "Wow. That must have been a pretty big accident," I said, looking at her leg.

"You should see my bike," Lisa said, laughing. "So what happened to you?"

"Soccer mess up," I said, blushing a little. I didn't want to get into it. "So, when can you play again?"

Lisa's smile drooped. "I'm out for the whole season. My one chance to take our team to state, and I blew it."

Suddenly being out for two weeks didn't seem so bad. I noticed a stack of CDs next to her bed. On top was Shauna Ferris's latest.

"Oh, my gosh!" I said. "Do you like Shauna Ferris?"

"She's my favorite singer," Lisa said, smiling.

"Me too!" I squealed. Lisa and I had a lot in common. It was nice to talk to somebody since my own friends were being so mean to me.

"My favorite thing to do after school is put on my Shauna CDs and play with my cat, Meow Mix. Do you like animals?" Lisa asked.

"Sure," I mumbled. Okay, so we didn't have everything in common.

"Anyway," Lisa went on. "I listen to Shauna Ferris all the time. She's awesome."

"You know, my mom knows her," I blurted. I wanted Lisa to know I wasn't just some silly sixth grader who'd barged into her room. I was cool.

Lisa sat up. "Your mom knows Shauna Ferris?"

"Yeah. Well, she knows Shauna's lawyer."

"Have you ever met her?" Lisa asked, like she was seriously impressed. "Do you think I could meet her?"

"Um. Sure. I'm sure my mom could set it up," I told her.

Lisa let out a squeal. "I'm going to meet Shauna Ferris! Arielle, this is the best thing that's ever happened to me. Thanks a ton!"

Okay, I hadn't actually said that I could arrange for Shauna Ferris to come and visit Lisa in the hospital. But doing something nice for Lisa was a perfect way to show my parents what a good person I really was. Why not?

"It's no biggie," I said, like I met celebrities every day.

If Mom could talk to Shauna's lawyer, I was sure Shauna would come visit Lisa. Stars did that kind of stuff all the time, and Shauna was so cool, she'd do it for sure. I was beginning to like the idea more and more.

A crackly voice came over the hospital paging system. "Arielle Davis, please report to the front desk."

"Sounds like they're paging you," Lisa said.

"Must be Mom," I said, hopping across Lisa's room to where I'd left my crutches. "Will you still be here on Friday?"

Lisa pointed to the big pulley thing holding up her leg. "Where else would I be?"

"See you Friday, then. Maybe I can bring some of my friends here to meet you." *If they're still my friends*, I thought. "Hang in there." I glanced at her leg. "Oops. Sorry."

Lisa laughed. Out in the bright hallway I hopped happily toward the lobby and my brand-new image: Arielle Davis, nice girl.

chapter
EIGHT

How to Get Shauna Ferris to Visit

1. Post messages on the IloveShauna.com site.
2. Fax a "searching for Shauna" request to the radio stations.
3. Beg Mom for help.
4. Look through Mom's Palm Pilot for numbers.
5. Put Traci, Felicia, and Amanda on it.

When I left Lisa's room and got to the lobby, I didn't see Mom anywhere. Instead I heard Felicia's voice.

"Hi, Arielle."

I turned around to see Felicia, Amanda, and Traci standing together.

"Hi," I said coolly. "What are you guys doing here?" I really wanted to tell them all about Lisa and my Shauna Ferris idea, but I wasn't sure if we were going to make up yet or not.

Felicia explained. "Your mom's still at the golf course. So we're kidnapping you. She said it was okay."

74

"I thought you were all mad at me," I said, without budging.

"We are. Well, we were," Amanda said. "But we miss you. We're willing to make up if you are."

Part of me didn't want to give in. Amanda *had* called me selfish. And Traci and Felicia hadn't exactly been nice to me, either. But I guessed I'd been a little crabby to them, too. I had started to say I was sorry when I remembered them whispering about me.

"Okay," I said. "I'm sorry, too. But I don't like it when you whisper about me behind my back."

"You totally took it the wrong way," Traci piped up. "We were talking about asking you out for pizza to make up when you stormed off. That's all."

I felt sort of silly now.

"So *are* we going for pizza?" I asked. I suddenly realized that I was starving.

Amanda smiled. It was so great to see her smile at me again. "Definitely. My stepmom is waiting to take us."

"So how did it go in physical therapy?" Felicia asked, taking my backpack for me.

"Okay. It hurts a little. Mr. Thompson is nice, though. He lets me call him Ray."

"Was it totally boring having to wait around here?" Felicia asked, taking in the nearly empty waiting room.

Boring? Meeting Lisa had been the best part of my day.

"No, it was great. I'll tell you all about it at the pizza place," I told them. "Come on, I really am starving!"

Traci laughed and opened the door for me. "Me too! Let's get going. There's a large pepperoni-and-pineapple pizza calling our names."

We got the last booth at Wonder Lake Pizza, and by the time Sal, the owner, dropped off our yummy pie, we were having a great time.

"Arielle, pass the garlic, please," Felicia said. I wrinkled my nose and passed it to her.

"I can't wait to get to the animal shelter," Traci said between bites of pizza.

Felicia turned to me. "My dad just got three new puppies yesterday and a baby bunny."

"I love bunnies," Traci said excitedly. "They're the cutest!"

Animal talk again. I wanted to keep the peace, though, so I said, "Sounds great," and grabbed another slice of pizza. It tasted extra good today.

"We'll have to get a move on if we want to make it to the shelter before six," Amanda chimed in.

Wait. We were actually going there *now*? I had only signed on for pizza. "Do we have to?" I said. I really didn't feel like going. I wanted to hang out with them and do something *I* liked to do, like shop at the mall or watch a movie.

Felicia looked down at her plate. "But I really want you to come with us, Arielle. You haven't met Grits yet. I just know you'll love him."

"Come on, Arielle," Amanda said, nudging me on the arm gently. "It'll be fun. You can feed him."

I rolled my eyes. "Okay. But next time we're going shopping." Traci and Amanda laughed. Felicia blew bubbles in her soda and slurped up the last few sips. I was so glad we were getting along again. I guess it pays to be nice.

"Anybody want more soda?" Felicia asked, raising her empty glass.

"Sure," I said, handing her my almost empty one. She walked over to the soda station for refills.

"Hey," Amanda said, going for her third piece of pizza. "We've got that vocab quiz tomorrow. I could come over to study with you after dinner tonight."

"Sure," I said. "Sounds great. Hey, Traci, how'd it go in soccer practice today?" I wondered if I'd missed a lot more new stuff.

"Good," she answered happily.

"Did you score any goals?" I asked breezily.

Traci looked down at her plate. "Two," she said quietly.

"Oh," was all I said. I didn't want Traci to be better than me. I wanted to be the Muskrats' best player and go to all-state, like Lisa Marconi. Lisa. I still hadn't told them about Lisa.

"More soda," Felicia chirped. She put my glass down in front of me.

"I have to tell you about this girl I met today at the hospital," I said.

"Did you meet her at physical therapy?" Traci asked, dabbing at some pizza sauce on her white shirt with a napkin. She's a good soccer player, but she's a total klutz with food.

I couldn't exactly tell them that I'd met Lisa while trying to avoid Felicia. "No, but she's a patient there. She's a center forward with the Tigers, or was, until she had a bike accident and broke her leg really badly. Now she's in traction and out for the whole season."

"That's awful." Felicia gasped. "My uncle was in traction after a motorcycle accident once. He had to just lie there for three months."

"I could never sit still for that long. I'd go crazy." Traci shook her head.

"I really want to do something nice for her. She's really cool," I added.

"She definitely sounds like she could use some major cheering up," Amanda said.

"Why don't we bring her to the animal shelter?" Felicia offered.

"Hello? She's in traction?" I reminded her.

"Oh, right."

"What about renting tons of movies for her?" Traci added.

"Or books from the Wonder Lake library?" Amanda was getting in on the action now. But hello? Books? How boring.

"I've already got a killer idea," I told them. "I'm going to get Shauna Ferris to come visit her. Isn't that awesome?"

Amanda, Traci, and Felicia stared at me with their mouths open—not a pretty sight if you're mid–pizza chew.

"How?" Felicia asked.

"Remember, my mom knows Shauna's lawyer."

Traci looked confused. "But isn't your mom really mad at you? I thought she took all your Shauna stuff."

She had a point.

Felicia joined in. "After all, Shauna's the reason you skipped practice in the first place."

Amanda leaned across the table for another slice of pizza. "Besides, if it was so easy to meet Shauna Ferris, don't you think you would have met her by now?"

I couldn't believe my friends were putting my idea down so fast. "You don't think I can do it?"

No one said anything. Felicia pretended to be interested in blotting her pizza grease. Traci chewed silently. Finally Amanda put her arm around me.

"It's a great idea, really, Arielle. But maybe we can come up with something more realistic. Something we can all do together?" she said.

"I'm in!" Felicia chirped.

"Me too," Traci added.

"No," I said, pulling away from Amanda's arm. "I can do this. I know I can." I had to do it. I'd promised Lisa. And I had to prove that I wasn't the selfish person everyone thought I was.

Amanda sighed. "Arielle . . ."

"Fine. I'll do it by myself. You'll see. And maybe I'll even introduce Shauna to my so-called friends. Maybe."

"It's not that we don't think it's a good idea. It's just that Shauna Ferris is a major star, and she's probably really busy. It's going to be really hard to get in touch with her," Felicia said.

"I can pull it off." I sniffed.

"But what if you can't?" Traci asked.

Felicia shredded her napkin into little bits. "Then Lisa would be getting her hopes up for nothing."

Amanda nodded. "I think you better tell Lisa the truth. Before she gets too excited about it."

"No way," I said, crossing my arms.

I'd show them. And my parents. And Lisa. And myself.

Amanda crossed her arms, too. "That is just plain irresponsible, Arielle Davis! And selfish."

She'd used my last name again. And she'd called me selfish. It was becoming a habit.

I looked to Traci and Felicia for support, but they kept quiet. I got up from the booth.

"Arielle, where are you going?" Felicia said.

"I'm calling my mom to come pick me up."

Traci frowned. "Aren't you going with us to the animal shelter?"

"No. I have to get started if I want to get in touch with Shauna Ferris," I said, looking right at Amanda.

"Fine," Amanda replied coolly. "See you later."

"Yeah, see you later," I said, hobbling toward the pay phone at the back.

I called Dad's office, and he said he'd pick me up in twenty minutes. I sat on the curb out front, waiting for him, trying not to cry. My friends didn't believe in me. Worse, they thought I was a selfish liar. They would all be surprised when I got Shauna Ferris to visit Wonder Lake. I was on a mission, and no one could stop me.

Not even Shauna Ferris herself.

chapter
NINE

Dear Diary,

   Me and my big mouth. Why did I have to tell Lisa
I could introduce her to Shauna Ferris? Shauna is
impossible to get in touch with. And no one will help
me. But I can't let Lisa down. I just can't. What am I
going to do?

I was starting to hate the name Shauna Ferris. I'd
spent hours on Shauna Web sites from Wonder Lake
to Australia. No one knew of any way to contact
Shauna other than writing to her record label, which
was pointless because she got millions of fan letters
every day. One girl had posted pictures of herself
with Shauna. She'd met her through a contest. But
unless there was a contest for injured soccer stars,
that wasn't going to help, either.

   I crashed on my bed and stared at my room: my white
bedspread with the green embroidered flowers that my
parents bought in France, the bookshelves with rows of
neatly stacked books, my limited-edition Mademoiselle
Rothschild dolls standing on top of my antique dresser.

All my Shauna posters were gone. There were little thumbtack marks in the walls where they had been. I knew Mom wasn't going to like it, but I was going to have to ask her for help. There was no other way.

"Mom?" I knocked on the door of her study.

"Hi, honey." She was sitting in her leather chair, reading a law book. She had on her reading glasses and the same peach silk suit she'd worn to work. At least she'd put on her slippers. That was about as relaxed as she got.

"Hi, princess." Dad was on the computer, typing away. I hadn't expected to talk to both of them, and it sort of threw me. I needed to tackle this sensibly, like a lawyer.

"Mom, Dad, I'd like you to consider the story of Lisa."

They looked at each other like their only child had gone wacko. "Who?" Dad asked.

"Lisa is a seventh-grade girl lying in traction at Wonder Lake Hospital right now while we enjoy all the comforts of home." I looked up at my parents. I had them. They were listening. "Lisa spends her days waiting and wishing for something to happen, something cool."

Dad raised his hand. "I ask again, who is Lisa?"

He was breaking my flow. "Dad." I sighed. "She's a girl I met at the hospital. She's so great. You would love her. Can I finish?"

Dad nodded. "Proceed, counselor." Dad always called me counselor when I tried to talk like a lawyer.

"I have a feeling there's a big finish coming," Mom said, and closed her book.

"There's only one thing in the world that Lisa wants—just one thing that would make her happy."

"Here it comes," Mom said.

My heart beat like a thousand drums. *Please, please, please let this work*, I prayed. "To meet Shauna Ferris." I said it in one big whoosh.

"I object," Mom said, standing up and whipping off her reading glasses.

I started rambling at warp speed. "But Mom, she's really bored there and I just want to cheer her up and I sort of told her that you knew Shauna's lawyer and—"

"You what?" Uh-oh. Mom was really upset.

"Arielle, you had no right to do that," Dad joined in.

"But Dad . . ."

"But nothing, Arielle." Mom paced back and forth in front of me. "I don't know what's gotten into you. Shauna Ferris is the whole reason you're wearing an Ace bandage right now."

"Exhibit A," Dad said, gesturing to my leg.

Mom went on. "You lied to us. That's a very serious offense, young lady."

Dad leaned back in the swivel chair and pushed away from his computer. "I don't suppose this would have anything to do with a certain young lady in this room wanting to meet her favorite singer, would it?"

"No way, Dad," I insisted. "This is totally about Lisa. I promise."

"You told us you went to soccer practice on Monday, so you'll forgive me if I don't completely trust everything you say right now, Arielle," Mom said.

"Please, Mom? I'll never ask for anything ever again."

Mom walked over to the bookcase, tousling my hair along the way and pulling it out of its scrunchie. It was her I'm-mad-but-I-still-love-you move. She pulled another law book off of the bookshelf. "If you want to cheer her up, why don't you buy her a nice card or some magazines?"

"Objection!" I said firmly. "On the grounds that that would be totally lame."

Dad couldn't help smiling. "Objection overruled, counselor."

"Please, Mom?" I begged.

"I know this is hard for you, Arielle. But the answer has to be no."

Dad shrugged. "Sorry, kid. Nice try, though."

All my frustration built into a torrent I couldn't hold back. "But you have to help me!" I shouted. Big mistake.

Mom shot me a glance over the top of her glasses. "Excuse me?"

"I sort of, um, promised Lisa you would do it," I admitted.

85

Mom put both hands on her hips. "Well, I guess you'll just have to unpromise her."

I didn't think *unpromise* was a word, but my English grades weren't exactly good enough for me to be correcting anyone's grammar.

"Fine! Go ahead and let Lisa down. I hope you can both sleep tonight, knowing that you've dashed a young girl's dreams to about a gazillion pieces." I turned to make a dramatic exit and tripped over Mom's leather ottoman. The doorbell rang, and I eagerly hopped down the stairs to get it. It was Amanda. She'd come over to give me my grammar lesson.

"Hi," she said, holding her book tight against her chest.

"Hi," I said back.

"Who is it, honey?" Mom shouted down the stairs.

"It's Amanda," I yelled back. "We're going to study for our vocabulary quiz."

"Okay," she answered, and then it was quiet.

I didn't know what was worse—studying with Amanda while we were mad at each other or knowing that I'd just lost my best chance of getting to Shauna Ferris.

"So, how's it going with the Shauna Ferris thing?" Amanda asked, plopping onto the couch.

"Okay." I shrugged. I couldn't admit that everything I'd tried had been a total disaster.

Amanda started to ask me another question, but I changed the subject. "Want some microwave pop-corn?"

She shrugged like she didn't care either way. "Sure."

I brought in a big bowl of the stuff, hopping around on one foot. And then we cracked the books. I couldn't concentrate, though. Big, ugly words stared up at me and did a polka around my head. Nothing sank in.

"What does *serendipity* mean?" Amanda looked at me with hope.

My brain went on scan. Nothing. "Oh, wait, is that the members-of-two-parties thing?"

Amanda's shoulders sagged. "No. That's *bipartisan*. *Serendipity* means 'the gift of finding valuable or agree-able things not sought for.' Like a happy surprise."

"Like I will ever use that word in my day-to-day life. Please," I said, rolling my eyes.

Amanda wasn't giving me an inch. "Arielle, if you don't want another C-minus, you're going to have to try a little harder."

"I am trying," I said defensively. "Give me another one."

"Okay," she said. "What does *unfortunate* mean?"

"*Unfortunate*," I answered confidently. "'Attended with misfortune.'" Hey, I'd gotten one right!

"Great. Now make a sentence with it," Amanda instructed.

It is unfortunate that my mom won't help me find Shauna Ferris, I thought.

"It's unfortunate that I have to wear this stupid bandage for two weeks."

"Not bad," Amanda said. "Next word: *treacherous*."

"Those are treacherous waters up ahead. Be sure to wear your life jacket," I said.

I looked at the next word. *Ignominious*. Meaning, 1. dishonorable, 2. despicable, 3. humiliating and degrading. *I will be ignominious if I let Lisa and my friends down*. Forget it—I couldn't study anymore.

"This is silly," I said, closing my book. "I won't need any of this stuff when I'm a famous lawyer/soccer player/rock star. I'll hire people to do it for me while I sing, meet with the Supreme Court, and compete in the Olympics."

"Even rock stars have to talk to the public. Think how cool you'll be when you use words like *cytoplasm* in interviews," Amanda said with a smile.

"Ugh. I don't even want to know that word," I said.

"It does sound pretty gross." Amanda giggled. The ice was thawing, and we were acting more like friends. I leaned back on the overstuffed sofa and let my legs dangle over the arm. Amanda put her head against mine and dangled her legs over the other arm. It's what we used to do when we were little kids. It felt good, her head pressing against mine. I missed all the stuff we used to do together. I missed the way we always got along. I was the leader, and Amanda liked to follow. Now it was different. She wore different clothes and spoke out more. Part of me wondered how I was supposed to act now that she was friends with Traci and Felicia. Did Amanda still need me?

"So, do you think I can ace the quiz tomorrow?" I asked.

"I think you'll do a lot better on tomorrow's quiz than you did on the other one," Amanda answered. It wasn't exactly the answer I was looking for.

"I want to get an A," I said.

Amanda bonked her head against mine. "You don't have to be the best at everything, you know. You just have to know how to use *treacherous* in a sentence. No big deal."

"I think I am in a treacherous position." I giggled and rolled off the sofa onto the carpet.

"Hey, that was good," Amanda said. She rolled onto the floor beside me, and we lay there giggling, neither one of us leading or following.

For the first time since I'd skipped soccer practice, things felt normal again. All it took was a little popcorn, some vocabulary, and a good giggle with my best friend. If only I could fix everything else as easily.

chapter
TEN

Instant Message from FlowerGrl to PrincessA

My baby-sitter is picking you up after your physical therapy. Guess your parents are really busy. We'll see you at the shelter, okay? A

"Push yourself, Arielle! You can do it!" Ray cried.

It was Monday afternoon, and I'd already done about a thousand lunges on my bad leg. My whole body was shaking. I couldn't wait to stop.

Ray must have read my mind. "That's a wrap, Arielle. Keep working like that, and you'll be on the soccer field again by next week."

That was the best news I'd heard in days. "Really? You mean it?"

"I mean it. You're doing great."

I was so happy, nothing could bring down my mood. At least, I thought nothing could. I hopped down the hall on my way to the lobby. But when I got to Lisa's room, I stopped cold. I still hadn't had any luck getting in touch with Shauna. In fact, I felt so bad about it, I avoided visiting Lisa on Friday. What could I tell her? Would she completely hate my guts? I hopped quietly past her open door, hoping she wouldn't see me. No such luck.

"Arielle! Where have you been?" Lisa waved to me from her hospital bed. I stood in the doorway, completely at a loss for words.

"Hey, where were you last Friday?" Lisa chided. "I had my mom bring in my latest stack of teen magazines. I thought we'd flip through them together."

"Sorry," I mumbled. "I, um, I had to go home and . . . clean my room. You know how moms are," I said, rolling my eyes for emphasis.

"So, have you talked to Shauna yet? What day is she coming?" Lisa asked me.

My heart skipped a beat. "Um, not yet," I croaked. *Tell her. Just tell her the truth, Arielle.* "It's just that . . . um, she's busy working on a new video, so it's kind of tough to get in touch with her right now."

"Oh." Lisa looked down and twirled her hospital bracelet around on her thin wrist.

My heart beat a message to my brain: *You are such a liar.* My mouth ignored it. "But it'll happen. My mom already talked to her agent and everything. It's just a matter of, you know, working out the schedules and stuff."

Lisa sat up. "Excellent! You are so cool, Arielle. I

told all my friends from the Tigers about you."

"Y-you did?" I stammered.

"Yeah. It's so great that you're doing this for me. And I really want to give you something, too," she said.

"Oh, that's okay," I said, reaching for my crutches so I could go.

Lisa reached into her bedside table and pulled out a green braided friendship bracelet. "I made this myself. We all wear them. It's kind of a team thing. But I made yours in a different color so your team wouldn't get upset. It'll look great on you."

She slipped the bracelet over my hand. It did look great, but I had never felt worse.

"Wow. Thanks so much. Look, I really have to go. My friend Amanda's baby-sitter is picking me up, and I don't want her to get worried." I laughed loudly. It sounded fake and nervous.

"Sure," Lisa said, sounding disappointed. "Didn't you say you were going to bring your friends by sometime to hang out?"

"Uh, yeah!" I chirped. But I didn't want the girls to meet Lisa until I knew for sure about Shauna. Otherwise they might say something and ruin everything. "Maybe next time."

"Right. And who knows. Next time I see you, you might bring Shauna Ferris!" Her mouth broke into a huge grin as she plopped back against the white hospital pillows.

"Yeah," I mumbled, wondering how I'd ever gotten myself into such a mess. "Maybe."

Amanda's baby-sitter, Penny, was waiting for me in the lobby, holding her purse and her car keys in one hand. She was wearing embroidered jeans and a beaded tank top. She's the one Amanda gets her seventies fashion sense from.

"Hi, Arielle. How did it go today?" Penny said.

"Fine," I lied. I was in a record bad mood after seeing Lisa. Oh, what had I done?

"Well, the girls are all waiting for you at the shelter. I'll bet you can't wait to see all those adorable puppies," Penny said cheerfully.

Right.

Fifteen minutes later we were pulling onto the dirt road that led to Mr. Fiol's house and the animal shelter. Traci and Amanda were sitting on the ground in front of Felicia's house. Traci was holding a small fur ball in her hands and rubbing her face against it.

"Cute kitten," I said cheerily as I got out of the car.

"Yeah," Traci said, without looking up. "She's a real sweetie." Felicia ran down from the house. She stopped when she saw me. Amanda and I had made up, but things were still going to be tense with Traci and Felicia, I guessed.

"How was your physical therapy?" Amanda asked.

"Okay," I said. "Ray says I'll be playing again by next week."

"That's great. You'll be scoring goals against the Tigers in no time," Amanda said, smiling at me.

Traci buried her nose in the kitten, pretending she wasn't listening, but I knew she was.

"We'll see," I said. Traci was good. And she'd had much more game time now than I had. What if Coach Talbot decided to make her center forward and keep me on the bench as her reliever?

Felicia finally decided to talk to me. "Would you like to see the new puppies? They're really cute."

"Sure," I said, trying to sound sunny and enthusiastic.

Felicia showed us back to the animal runs. Mr. Fiol took off his baseball hat and waved to us.

"My goodness. Did the Miss Teen America pageant let out early? Who are all these beautiful girls here to help out?"

Felicia rolled her eyes. "Dad. That is so corny."

"Did I ever tell you the one about the corn who ate too much?" Mr. Fiol asked, ignoring his daughter.

We played along. "No! What happened?" Amanda asked.

"He got so full, he popped! Get it? Popped corn?"

Felicia glanced at us, embarrassed. "Yeah, Dad. We got it."

Mr. Fiol's jokes were corny, but I liked him. He

could be pretty strict with Felicia, and he had a lot of rules, but he always had time for us.

"I better take that kitten inside and get her cleaned up. Someone's coming to take her in a little bit," Mr. Fiol said.

"That's so great," Traci said, handing the calico kitten over to him. But I could tell she wished she could take the cat home herself.

Mr. Fiol set off for the house, and we went into the runs to look at the dogs. There were five or six puppies frolicking in the grass. Three were white and brown, all from the same litter. One was gray and beige, with long hair like a small sheepdog. A fat, pug-nosed dog lay in the corner on some straw, chewing on a red toy.

"Hey. What are you doing?" A hyper little black pup was chewing at my Ace bandage. He licked between my toes, and it tickled like crazy. "Hey, stop that!"

"Isn't he great?" Felicia reached down and picked him up. He wasn't much bigger than her hands. "This is Grits."

The pup jerked forward and started licking my face. "Cut it out." I laughed.

"He's usually pretty shy. He must like you, Arielle," Traci said.

"He is kind of cute," I said. Before I knew it, I was holding him. His little body felt soft and warm.

Amanda put her hand to her forehead like she felt faint. "Uh-oh, don't look now, but Arielle is discovering dog love."

"You are a total loser, you know that?" I said, laughing.

Amanda sat down on the ground. Three white-and-brown puppies ran over and tackled her. "Save me! Save me." She giggled. "I'm being licked to death."

Traci and Felicia squealed and ran over to play with the puppies, too. I couldn't believe it. It was so third grade. And they were getting really dirty. But it looked like fun.

"Come on, puppy. Let's get in on the action. Make way for us," I screamed. I ran over and landed on my butt with a thud. The pug-nosed puppy brought me his chew toy. I grabbed one end while he tugged on the other with his mouth, growling in the cutest way.

"I think somebody's jealous," Felicia said.

Sure enough, the little black pup jumped into my lap and licked at my face till I had to let go of the chew toy so I could pet him.

We played with the puppies for half an hour. It was funny. I completely forgot what a bad mood I'd been in. I didn't think about anything. Not my leg. Not my parents. Not Shauna Ferris or Lisa. And then, sitting there with dog slobber on me, I had an idea.

"Time-out!" I called. "Hey, Felicia, do you have anything yummy to drink at your house?"

Felicia jumped up and dusted off her pants. "We have lemonade," she said.

"Do you mind if we have some?" I asked.

Felicia took us inside her kitchen. We sat at her kitchen table while she filled plastic cups with ice-cold lemonade. Photographs of animals that Felicia had taken care of were stuck all over the fridge. The kitchen wasn't anything like our newly remodeled kitchen with the real granite counters that came all the way from New York City. But it was cozy and clean.

"I have an amazing idea," I said. Traci shot Amanda a warning look. My cheeks got a little hot. I hadn't even told them my idea, and already Traci was ready to shoot it down.

"What is it?" Felicia asked. At least she wanted to hear it.

"Maybe we can bring a puppy to the hospital to cheer up Lisa. I mean, if those puppies can make me feel better, they've got to make her feel better. Right?"

Felicia brought out some cheese and crackers. "That's a great idea," she said. "I'm sure my dad would say okay."

"Some hospitals use pets as therapy for sick kids and stuff. It can actually help them get better," Amanda said. "I read about it in a magazine."

"What about Shauna Ferris?" Traci asked, moving her straw around in her lemonade.

I thought about the hours I'd spent on the Internet, getting nowhere fast. It had been a pretty far-fetched idea. But I didn't want anyone to think I'd failed. "Please," I huffed. "That idea is so five minutes ago. Pet therapy is where it's at."

Traci, Amanda, and Felicia all smiled at me.

"It's a great idea," Traci said. "I can't wait to get started."

"We'll need to get organized," Amanda said. She grabbed a pad and pen off the counter. "Who do we need to talk to at the hospital to make sure this is okay?"

"The hospital administrator, I think," Traci volunteered.

"Okay," Amanda continued. She jotted a note down on the pad. "Number one: talk to hospital administrator."

I opened my mouth, but Felicia was way faster. "Maybe we should make up some posters for it and put them all over the hospital so everyone knows we're coming. Amanda, you could do that. You're the best at art."

Amanda smiled. "Thanks, Felicia. And you could take some pictures of the dogs to put on the posters."

Felicia sounded really excited. "I've got some great pictures that I took last week. I used black-and-white film so they look artsy."

I cleared my throat. But Traci jumped in. "We've got to give them each a bath before we go."

"Definitely," Amanda agreed. She wrote down *bath* on the pad.

"What about a name?" Traci asked.

"Right! Our program needs a name. Something everyone can remember." Amanda chewed on the end of her pen, thinking.

"It needs to be something about getting well or healing. . . ." Traci was thinking out loud.

I couldn't think of anything.

"I know!" Felicia raised her hand like she was in class. "What about Healing Paws?"

"That's perfect," Traci said.

"I love it," Amanda agreed.

Nobody asked me.

Traci and Felicia started throwing out ideas, and Amanda kept writing them down. I hadn't seen them this excited since our fund-raiser for the shelter. I was starting to feel totally left out. After all, it was my idea in the first place. Now my friends were planning everything without me.

"Excuse me. Can I say something?" It came out a little meaner than I meant it to.

Amanda stopped writing. "Sure, Arielle." They all waited for me to speak. That's when I realized I didn't know what to say. I just wanted to be included. The name was fine, really. It wasn't like I had a better one.

I swallowed hard. "I want to talk to the hospital administrator," I said, and shrugged to make it look like it was no big deal. "I'm there for physical therapy twice a week, anyway."

Amanda wrote it down. "Sure. Arielle clears it with the hospital."

Felicia and Traci smiled. "Great," Traci said. "This is such a cool idea, Arielle."

It was a cool idea, but I hoped Lisa wouldn't be too disappointed that we were bringing in a bunch of dogs instead of Shauna Ferris.

After a few more minutes of planning I was bored.

"Let's go see the dogs again and tell them they're going on an adventure," I suggested.

Did I actually say that? Me, the girl who didn't like animals? What was happening to me?

The other girls looked shocked. And then we all ran outside, giggling. All the puppies were sleeping, except for the little black one. He came right up and started batting at my toes again. I laughed out loud and picked him up.

"Gosh, he really likes you, Arielle." Traci gave the pup a kiss on his head.

"He is pretty cute," I admitted, holding him up for inspection. "He looks so determined, like a fighter."

"Just like somebody else we know," Amanda said, nudging me in the ribs.

I held Grits up to my face. His nose was wet and cold against mine. He licked me right on the mouth, and I didn't even mind his dog breath. "Hey, Grits," I said, cuddling him in my arms. "How would you like to go see a friend of mine? I think she'll like you a lot."

Grits yawned and nuzzled my arm.

"I think that means yes," Traci said.

I couldn't wait to see Lisa's face when we brought him into her room. Maybe we'd put a big red bow around his neck. Finally I had a chance to do something right. And everyone would know I wasn't selfish.

Traci's eyes suddenly grew big. "I think you should probably put him down now."

Figured she'd be jealous that Grits liked me instead of her. I made a smoochy face at Grits. "Why should I put you down, Gritsy boy?"

"Because I think he has to *go*," Traci said.

"Oh, my gosh!" I put Grits down and jumped back about a foot.

Grits wagged his tail happily at me, and I smiled back down at him.

I guess we kind of found each other by accident. A happy accident.

Like, serendipity.

At least I'd gotten one word right on my vocab quiz.

chapter
ELEVEN

Paw-Print Stationery with Healing Paws _Written in Calligraphy at Top_

Arielle—
    Isn't Amanda's stationery amazing? Don't
forget—sleepover at my house tonight! Bring
comfy PJs and a sleeping bag. Mom promised
my annoying brother will stay in his room.
                              —Traci

"Mr. Chang will see you now, Miss Davis," the hospital secretary told me. I was sitting outside the hospital's administrative office, holding my Healing Paws poster, ready to convince Mr. Chang—the hospital's director—to let us bring the animals to the hospital.

"Thanks," I croaked.

She showed me into his office. A man in a suit and tie was standing behind a big wooden desk. He was about my dad's age.

"So this is Miss Davis? I'm Ned Chang. Nice to meet you." His handshake was solid and friendly, but his gray suit was all business. My stomach did a flip-flop.

"Nice to meet you, too," I said.

Mr. Chang took a seat behind his desk. "So what can I do for you today, Miss Davis?"

"W-w-well," I stammered. *Get control, Arielle. Think of Mom and Dad in the courtroom.* "Well, sir, Mr. Chang. I'd like to present to you exhibit A. The Healing Paws poster." I spread the poster out on his desk. Mr. Chang nodded at it and smiled. Beads of sweat popped out on my forehead. I tried to remember all the stuff Amanda had told me about pet therapy. "Many hospitals use pets as a form of therapy. It's a proven fact that pets can help people feel happier and calmer, and that helps them heal faster. And besides, they're totally cute."

Totally cute? *Come on, Arielle. Don't blow it.*

I scrambled for more lawyer talk, but I couldn't think of a thing to say. So I decided to talk to him the way I would to my friends.

"The thing is, there's a girl here, Lisa Marconi? She's in traction."

"Yes," Mr. Chang said. "I know Lisa. I hear she's quite the soccer player."

He knew her! He'd have to understand now.

"We just met a week ago, but I liked her right away. I really wanted to do something for her. My friend Felicia's dad runs an animal shelter. You

103

should see how happy it makes people just to come in and be around the animals. And that's when we got the idea." I was totally rambling now. I just had to get it out and over with. "Pet therapy. Healing Paws. It's all for Lisa. We just want her to get better and have fun."

I stood in front of his desk and waited for him to answer. Mr. Chang read over the proposal we'd written up. I could hear the clock ticking on his desk and the blood thumping in my head. He stuck his hand out to shake my hand. "It's a deal," he said.

"Yay!" I shouted, jumping up and down. I'm serious. It was like I was in kindergarten all of a sudden. *Control yourself, Arielle.*

Mr. Chang laughed. "I've got an even better idea," he said. "How about making this a regular program at the hospital? Say, once a month?"

Weird. When I wanted something from my parents, I always had to beg and plead. This was way too easy. No fighting. No whining. I guess that's what happens when you do something nice for someone else.

"I'm sure my friends would love that," I said eagerly. "Wait'll you see this one dog, Grits. He's my favorite."

Mr. Chang opened his desk drawer and pulled out a picture of three huge dogs lying in front of a fireplace. Dog toys were everywhere. "You don't have to convince me. I've got three of my own at home."

I couldn't wait to get home and tell the girls. Healing Paws was going to be a big success.

Mr. Chang showed me to the door. "So next Wednesday, after school. We'll see you at four o'clock. You can ask them to page me when you get to reception." His face turned serious. "Now, remember—this is a hospital filled with people trying to rest and get well. I expect you to be responsible and make sure everything runs smoothly."

I took a deep breath and looked Mr. Chang right in the eyes. "I promise," I said. And I meant it. This was one of the most important things I had ever done—no way did I want to mess up.

I knew I should stop by and see Lisa before I left the hospital, but I couldn't face telling her that Shauna wasn't coming. Plus I didn't want to spoil the surprise by telling her that I had something else planned. I felt a little bad, but she'd forgive me. It was going to be worth the wait.

On the ride over to Traci's house for our sleepover, I wanted to tell Mom all about Healing Paws. If I could prove that I was being responsible, maybe she'd give me back my Shauna CDs. A week and a half without listening to my music had been torture.

"Mom, I want to tell you something," I started.

A light drizzle spattered the windshield. Mom

hated driving in the rain. "These windshield wipers need a good tune-up," she muttered to herself.

"They're fine, Mom. It's hardly raining. That's the problem," I said.

"I think I'll ask your father to take the car into the shop. Now, what was it you wanted to tell me?" Mom asked.

"Well, when I was over at Felicia's dad's animal shelter, I had this idea—"

Mom interrupted. "Oh, dear. I forgot to tell Anya to pick up your dad's suits from the cleaners. He'll be furious."

"Mom?" I sighed.

"Yes?" she asked, like I hadn't started a conversation nearly three times.

"Nothing," I said. Obviously it wasn't the right time to tell her about our plans. That's all right—I could live without my Shauna music a little while longer.

We drove up in front of Traci's house, and I pulled my sleeping bag out of the backseat. It was the Princess Jera one that Mom had gotten for me at Christmas when they were the hottest thing around. Like, a million years ago.

"Mom, can I get a new sleeping bag, please?" I mumbled.

"Arielle! That's not even a year old yet."

"But it's so fifth grade," I whined. "Nobody's into Princess Jera anymore. It's embarrassing."

"We'll see," she said. "Have a good time tonight."

I lugged my stupid fairy princess sleeping bag up to Traci's door and rang the bell.

Traci's older brother, Dave, answered it, wearing a skateboarding T-shirt. So much for staying in his room.

"Hi," he said, opening the door wide. I wasn't on crutches anymore, but my leg was still bandaged. "Want me to carry that upstairs for you?" He pointed to my sleeping bag.

"Um, no thanks. I can get it," I said, pushing Princess Jera's face behind my back.

"I heard about your soccer blowout," Dave said. "Bummer. How's the physical therapy going?"

"Okay," I said. "You know."

"Yeah," he said, grinning. "I do know. That electrical-stimulation thingy is kind of cool, though."

"Yeah," I said. Traci made it sound like Dave was really obnoxious, but I could see why Amanda liked him. He was sweet.

Just then Traci appeared at the top of the stairs. "Come on up, Arielle. Guess what? Amanda brought her Shauna CDs!"

Yes! What Mom didn't know wouldn't hurt her.

Traci's room was plastered with animal posters, and there was a collection of horses on top of her dresser.

Amanda was sitting on Traci's floor, letting Felicia

braid glittery ribbons into her long hair. "How did it go?" Felicia asked.

"Fantastic," I said. I plopped my sleeping bag on the floor upside down, covering Princess Jera's face. "We're on for next Wednesday after school. And get this—Mr. Chang wants us to make it a regular program. He loved the idea!"

We all high-fived one another. It was really dorky, but it made us laugh.

I pulled a bottle of purple nail polish out of my overnight bag and began to paint my toenails. Traci started painting Amanda's toenails blue.

"I knew it was a good idea when I thought of it," I said.

Traci looked up. "Why do you have to take credit for everything, Arielle?" she asked.

I stopped midtoe. "It was my idea."

"But it took all of us to make it happen," Amanda said.

She was right. "Well, it doesn't really matter whose idea it was," I said, relenting. "I promised Mr. Chang we'd be responsible. We have to get organized."

"Right," Amanda said. She pulled out her pad and pen again. We could be on a deserted island, and Amanda would be making to-do lists. "Felicia, can you get dog treats and leashes from your dad?"

Felicia finished another braid on Amanda's hair.

"Sure. I'll bring some chew toys, too. That'll help us get them in and out of their carrying cases."

Amanda looked at me. "Arielle, you should probably make a little speech about Healing Paws so everyone knows why we're there."

I gulped. Hadn't I already done my part by meeting with Mr. Chang? "Uh . . . okay," I said.

"Great," Amanda said, checking something off on her list. "And Traci and I can be the dog wranglers."

We all picked a dog to be in charge of. I took Grits. He was my favorite. I couldn't wait to show him to Lisa.

Traci brought up some chips and soda.

Amanda munched a chip. "Hey, did you hear? Traci scored three goals in practice today."

Three goals? That was pretty major.

"Amanda," Traci said, trying to shush her. They all got quiet.

"That's great, Traci. Good going," I said, trying not to sound as jealous as I felt.

"Just a lucky day," Traci said, shrugging. "Hey, want me to show you the plays we've been practicing so you'll be ready to play on Friday?"

"Sure," I said nonchalantly. "As soon as my toes are dry."

Amanda changed the subject. "I turned in my application for student government today. Did anybody else do it? The deadline is Monday."

"I wish I could. But between orchestra and soccer, there's no way I could do government, too," Traci said.

"I can't, either. I need to be able to help my mom out at the bakery and my dad at the animal shelter," Felicia said.

"I'm still thinking about it," I said.

Amanda flipped her teen magazine open to a page full of cute guys. "I talked to Asher Bank all about it today. He is so nice. Not like most eighth graders, who won't talk to you because you're in sixth grade. Did you ever notice how long his eyelashes are?"

I burst out laughing. So did Traci and Felicia.

Amanda looked up. "What?" she demanded.

"You are totally crushing on Asher Bank," I said.

Amanda blushed deep red. "I am not!"

"And you're also the world's worst liar," I said.

Amanda rolled her eyes. "I'm joining student government because I want to make a difference, that's all."

"Sure," Felicia said.

"We believe you," Traci chimed in.

"Seriously!" Amanda looked at me. "Arielle, you believe me, right?"

I snatched the magazine from her hands. "Sure, I believe you," I said, not doing a very good job of hiding my smile.

I unrolled my sleeping bag and wriggled inside it. No one said anything about how immature it looked.

Traci pulled a soccer ball out from under her bed and stood over me with it.

"Miss Davis, if your toes are dry enough to get in that bag, they're dry enough to play soccer," she said, imitating Coach Talbot's serious tone.

Felicia finished braiding the last ribbon into Amanda's hair. "Come on," she said, rising to her feet. "We can all play."

"Oh, yeah?" I said. I scooted out of my bag, and the four of us ran down the stairs and out into Traci's yard to play barefoot soccer in the grass.

My toes got a little messed up, but I didn't mind. It felt great to have my friends back.

chapter
TWELVE

My To-Do List

1. Study vocab (like I'll ever need to use neurological in a sentence. Please.).
2. Do exercises Ray taught me (I have to play in our first game!).
3. Help Dad find his glasses.
4. Find my pink top.
5. Get wet-dog smell out of my favorite capri pants.

"Come on, Arielle. You can do better than that." It was another Monday and another day of physical therapy. I'd already done forty calf raises, and my poor calves were shaking.

"Can we stop now, Ray?" I whined. "I'm bored."

"Are you bored? Or are you just a wimp?"

No one calls me a wimp. I narrowed my eyes down to slits and gritted my teeth. "Forty-one, forty-two, forty-three . . ."

When I got to fifty, Ray clapped. "Good work. Now let's try some running moves."

"Do you think I should do running so soon, Ray?" I asked. What if I couldn't do it?

Ray laughed and cleared some weights out of the way. At the far end of the room I could see my reflection in the mirrored wall. I looked scared. "You could probably run a marathon if you wanted to. Okay. Toes on the line, and when I say 'go,' show me what you've got."

My heart was pounding.

"Ready . . . set . . . go!"

I took off down the length of the room and stopped at the wall. It didn't hurt at all. In fact, it felt pretty good.

"Well, that was okay," Ray said. "But I know you can do better. You were holding out on me."

"I was not," I huffed, even though I totally had been.

Ray crossed his arms, but he was still smiling. "You know, Arielle, sometimes people are afraid to go all out after they've been injured. They're afraid it'll hurt or that they'll find out they can't do what they used to do."

I frowned. "I'm not holding back. I just needed to warm up," I insisted.

Ray's eyes twinkled. "Oh, I know that. I just wanted to point out that some people feel that way, that's all."

"Well, I'm not some people," I said. I lined up again.

"Okay," said Ray. "On your mark, get set, go!"

We did five more sprints and then some stop-and-start action with the ball. Before long I'd totally forgotten to be scared and was completely focused on beating Ray to the ball.

"Time!" Ray caught the soccer ball and held up his hands in a time-out *T*. "I think you're healed."

"Really? You mean it?" I breathed.

"Uh-huh. This is officially your last physical therapy session. You're good as new."

I was so excited, I gave Ray a big hug. He laughed and hugged me back.

Ray walked me to the lobby to wait for my dad. "I'll look for your name in the headlines when I check out the local sports results."

I hoped he was right. I tried to smile, but I guess I didn't fake it very well.

"Don't be afraid to go for it, Arielle," Ray advised. "But don't go overboard, either. Just play your best."

I nodded and twirled the green friendship bracelet that Lisa had made me around my wrist. I'd gone days without stopping in to see her. She was probably pretty mad at me. I had to go talk to her. I took a deep breath for courage and walked over to her room. But she wasn't there.

A nurse came in to change the sheets. "She's down in

X ray right now. She'll be back in about ten minutes."

I'd be gone in ten minutes. "Um, can you tell her that Arielle says hi?" I asked the nurse.

"Sure," she said. "I'll tell her."

"Thanks," I said. I'd have to save that courage for another day. On the way out I stopped at the hospital card shop and bought a card with a big sunflower on it for Lisa. I was hoping to find one with a soccer ball on it or a picture of a dog, but they only had ones with flowers. It would have to do. Wednesday, I'd make it up to her.

Dad dropped me at the shelter on the way to his tennis lesson at the country club. Shrieks and giggles greeted me as I walked over to the animal runs. Traci, Amanda, and Felicia were giving the dogs a bath. On the ground were big buckets of soapy water, wet brushes, and sponges.

Felicia waved to me. Her red T-shirt was completely soaked. "Hi, Arielle! Look! Amanda got our shirts made." She pulled out the front of her shirt so I could read it: HEALING PAWS, it said, with a little picture of a paw next to a picture of a hand. Cute.

"Come help us!" Traci called as she chased a wet puppy across the grass. She slipped in the grass and came up a grass-stained, muddy mess.

Grits escaped from Felicia's hands and ran toward me. "Catch him, Arielle!" she cried.

"No way. I'm staying dry," I insisted.

"Come on, it's fun," Felicia said, lunging for the slippery puppy.

"Yeah, right," I said. There was no way I was getting all wet and dirty. Not even for Grits. "Guess what? Ray says I'm through with physical therapy. I can start playing soccer this week."

"That's great," Amanda said.

"I can't wait till you're back on the team again," Traci said. I couldn't tell what she meant by that. Did she miss having me around, or was she looking forward to showing off all the new moves she'd learned?

I acted cool. "Yeah, and he says I'm going to be better than ever." Traci didn't flinch.

"You'll be great," Felicia said. "Whoops!"

Just then Grits slipped away from her again. He made a break for me and shook his wet body all over, spraying me with doggy water.

"Gross!" I squealed. Grits jumped up on my legs. "You guys! He's ruining my new capri pants."

"Hey, Arielle." Felicia giggled. "We're supposed to give the dogs a bath, not the other way around."

"Very funny." I sighed.

Amanda laughed and pointed. "Look, Grits is making his own Healing Paws design on your pants."

Enough was enough. I spied a bucket of cold water near the pump. "Who said they wanted a bath?" I tossed the water over Felicia's head. She screamed and jumped up and down when the cold water whooshed down her shirt.

"No way!" Felicia cried. She grabbed a dirty wet sponge and threw it at me, soaking my shirt.

Amanda and Traci stared.

"Oops," Felicia squeaked.

"Now you're really in for it," I growled. I tackled her and squeezed the soapy sponge over her head. Then Amanda and Traci joined in, dumping another bucket of water over us. We were all laughing so hard, we couldn't stand up.

"Come on," I said when I got my breath back. "Let's get these dogs looking gorgeous."

I have to say that nothing is funnier than trying to catch a wet dog—except trying to catch three wet dogs. Grits gave me the most trouble. I'd get him all scrubbed down, and then he'd run right for the mud again. Finally I held him in my lap and gave him— and me—the bath of a lifetime. When it was over, I stuck him inside his pen on a nice warm towel. He whimpered pitifully at me.

"Sorry, pal, this is for your own good." I started to walk away, and he whimpered even louder. I could never understand why people got all mushy about whimpering dogs. Now I got it.

"I'll be back later. I promise," I said, sticking my face into the cage for a few good licks. I gave him his chew toy and went back for more dog bath action.

"I hope the dogs look better than you four do!" Mr. Fiol said, watching us from the patio.

"Hi, Dad." Felicia giggled.

"I think we need a picture of this," Mr. Fiol called. He dashed into the house and came back with his camera.

"We can put this up on the shelter's bulletin board," he said, squinting into the lens.

Not in my lifetime.

"Okay, everybody get together and say 'Healing Paws.'"

Amanda was up in a flash. She put her arm around Felicia and Traci. They looked like soggy laundry hanging on a clothesline.

"Arielle, stand next to me." Felicia patted her side.

"I'll pass," I said.

Mr. Fiol wasn't going for it. "You've never looked better, Arielle. I promise." He put the camera up to his face and waited.

"Please, Arielle," Amanda whispered. "For us?"

"Okay." I sighed. I walked over and put my arm around Felicia.

"Say 'Healing Paws,'" Mr. Fiol shouted.

We all screamed together, *"Healing Paws!"*

I'm sure I looked really scary. But I'd never felt better.

chapter
THIRTEEN

Card to Lisa Marconi, Wonder Lake Hospital

Dear Lisa,

   Sorry about the corny card. And sorry I haven't been around more. I dropped by Monday, but you were in X ray—did the nurse tell you I was there? Hope everything is okay. And get ready for a big surprise on Wednesday, 'kay?

                                    Love, A

P.S. Are you totally psyched? Curious? DTK? (dying to know)

P.P.S. Hi, Lisa! We've heard a lot about you. Can't wait to meet you. See you soon. Amanda, Felicia & Traci (Arielle's buds)

"It's okay, Grits," I said, looking in through the metal door of the blue carrying case as I carried him up the hospital steps. Grits yawned and tried to lick my nose through the bars. He wasn't nervous, but I was.

"Hi, girls. Welcome to Wonder Lake Hospital," Mr. Chang said when he met us in the lobby. I introduced everybody, including Grits.

Mr. Chang peered into Grits's carrying case and talked to him in a funny, baby-talk voice. Grits wagged his tail back. Then Mr. Chang put his hand on my shoulder. "This is a great thing you're doing, girls."

He ushered us into the sunny playroom in the children's ward. Six kids sat in a clump by the windows. Staff members and parents lined the walls.

"Oh, look, how cute!" a nurse said, pointing at Grits.

"Hello, everyone," Mr. Chang said. "I'd like to introduce Arielle, Traci, Amanda, and Felicia of Healing Paws. This is a very special program. Since you haven't been able to see any animals for a while, Healing Paws brings the animals to you. Girls?"

Felicia lifted a wiry, beige mutt out of her cage. "This is Mabel. She's kind of funny looking, but she loves be petted."

Next Amanda brought out a tiny black kitten with a white nose. "This is Mr. Big." A couple of kids laughed at that.

Traci showed off Boxer, a cute white pup with a brown streak. "Boxer likes to eat," she told them. "He'll eat anything."

And then I introduced Grits. "He's kind of hyper-active," I said. "But he's really sweet, too."

The kids took turns petting, holding, and playing with the puppies and kitten. The way they laughed and shrieked, it was hard to believe they were sick. A little girl who'd just had surgery on her arm took a big lick in the face from Grits. One of the nurses held a little boy on her lap while he jangled a bell on a string in front of the kitten.

I noticed a little boy sitting by himself in the corner.

"Hey, Traci, can I borrow Boxer for a sec?" I asked.

"Sure," she said, handing him over.

"Hi," I said, sitting down beside the boy with Boxer in my arms. "What's your name?"

He had huge brown eyes. I guessed he was about five. "Jasper," he answered in a froggy whisper.

"Jasper, this is Boxer." I put Boxer in Jasper's lap, and he went to work right away, licking and sniffling and snuffling him. Jasper giggled and rumpled Boxer's ears. In a few minutes Boxer settled down in Jasper's lap like they were old friends and promptly went to sleep.

"He really likes you," I said.

"He's nice," Jasper said. "I had an operation on my throat."

"You did?"

"Yup. I get to eat a lot of ice cream."

A woman with dark hair pulled into a bun came

and sat with us. "Mommy!" Jasper croaked. "Look!"

"Who do you have here?" Jasper's mom asked. Jasper told her all about Boxer and how nice he was.

"Can we take Boxer home with us?" Jasper asked.

"Well, Jasper, your birthday was last month," she said, frowning thoughtfully. She glanced at me and smiled. "But Boxer could be your extra-special late birthday present," she added.

Jasper beamed back at her and whispered excitedly in the puppy's ear. "Did you hear that, Boxer? I'm bringing you home!"

Mr. Chang joined us. "Arielle? Do you have a few words about Healing Paws that you'd like to share?"

Suddenly I was nervous again. I stood up and cleared my throat.

"Hi, everybody. Thanks for making our first day with Healing Paws so great. The whole idea behind Healing Paws is that hanging out with animals is good therapy because it makes people smile."

A male nurse called out, "Are you going to do this again?"

I looked at my friends, who all nodded back at me. "Definitely," I said.

Traci jumped up. "And you can always volunteer at the animal shelter," she declared.

"Or make a donation to the shelter," Amanda added.

"And all these puppies are up for adoption," I said.

"Well, all except for one." I nodded at Jasper, and he smiled back.

Mr. Chang put his hands on his hips and raised both eyebrows. "Are you finished? Do you want to organize a food drive and a peace summit while you're at it?"

Everyone laughed. Healing Paws was a major success. Usually I only felt that good after I'd scored a goal or bought myself the best outfit in the mall. Somehow this felt even better.

But I still had one more thing to do.

I picked up Grits and cuddled him in my arms. "Come on," I told my friends. "Let's go surprise Lisa."

The four of us made our way down the hall to Lisa's room. I was nervous again. What if Lisa hated me for not bringing Shauna? Or for not visiting her in so long?

Traci took Grits, and I knocked lightly on Lisa's door.

"Come in," she said.

I stuck my head into the room. "Hi," I said.

Lisa was reading a soccer magazine. "Hi," she said, her eyes distrustful. "Where have you been?"

I swallowed hard. "Um, sorry. I'll explain everything. I brought that surprise. Can we come in?"

Lisa sat up. "I guess," she said. She didn't sound like she really wanted to see me or like she really cared about my surprise.

I turned around to take Grits from Traci, and we all walked in together.

"Lisa, these are my friends Amanda, Traci, and Felicia," I said. They all waved and said hi. "And this is Grits."

I plopped him down onto her bed, and immediately a huge smile lit up Lisa's face. "Oh, wow, he is the cutest thing ever!" She rubbed Grits's ears and looked up at me. "Where did you get him?"

I took a deep breath and told her all about Healing Paws and the crazy dog-bath water fight and Mr. Chang. Then I told her the truth about Shauna Ferris.

I pulled my one-of-a-kind Shauna T-shirt out of my bag and handed it to her. "I know it's not the same as meeting her, but I wanted you to have this."

Lisa fingered the T-shirt. Grits sniffed her hair and pawed at the pillow behind her head.

A big, tight lump sat in my throat. "Are you mad at me?" I asked.

"Yeah, kind of," Lisa answered. "I mean, I'm disappointed about Shauna and all. But that's not what I'm mad about. I wish you'd just been honest with me."

"I know," I said, picking at my fingernails. "I just wanted you to like me."

Lisa's eyebrows furrowed. "I wouldn't have made you a friendship bracelet if I didn't like you, Arielle." Then she smiled. "I think it's great that you made this

124

whole Healing Paws thing happen, though. It's so cool and so . . ." She searched for a word. "Unselfish."

Unselfish? Had someone actually used the words *un* and *selfish* about *me* in the same sentence?

I leaned forward and gave Lisa a hug. "Thanks!"

Grits leaped into Lisa's lap, barking and wagging his tail.

"I think he likes you." Amanda laughed.

"You think so?" Lisa asked.

Grits licked her face.

"Definitely," Traci and Amanda said together.

"Do you think I could adopt him?" Lisa asked.

"Absolutely!" Felicia said. "I can call my dad as soon as we leave and fix it up for you."

"Well, I have to ask my parents first, but what do you think, Arielle, do you think I should?" Lisa nuzzled her nose in Grits's soft fur.

"Sure," I said, a little sadly. I'd miss Grits, but he was going to have a great home. "When are you getting out of here?"

"Well," Lisa said. "You haven't noticed my big change."

"Your big change?" I looked around the room. Suddenly it hit me. "Oh, wow! No more traction!"

"That's right. I'll be walking out of here this Friday. On crutches, but hey, at least it's walking."

"That's great!" Traci said. "Friday? Oh, my gosh, you have to come to our soccer game."

"I'm already coming," she announced. "But I play for the Tigers, remember? Sorry, but I'll be cheering for the other team."

"Well, no offense, Lisa," I said, glancing at Traci. "But we plan to kick some serious Tiger butt."

"We'll see," Lisa said. Grits licked her face, and Lisa giggled. It felt so great to see her smile.

A nurse came in with a pitcher of juice. "Well, who do we have here?" she asked, smiling at Grits.

"My new dog," Lisa said happily.

Felicia pulled her camera from her purse. "Excuse me," she asked the nurse shyly. "But would you mind taking a picture of all of us?"

At least I wasn't covered in dog fur for this one. We all sat on the bed, surrounding Lisa and Grits. The nurse snapped our picture.

"Perfect," she said.

chapter
FOURTEEN

Flyer Posted All Over WLMS

The Wonder Lake Muskrats
vs.
the Silver Lake Tigers.
Friday, 4:00 P.M. WLMS Playing Field.
Go, Muskrats!

"Pass your papers to the front, please." Mrs. Scott stood at the front of the class with outstretched hands. I passed mine forward with a little groan.

"How'd you do?" Amanda whispered.

"I don't know. I think I did okay. I got a little confused on that whole semicolon, no-semicolon thing. But I felt good about the vocab part."

"Me too," Amanda said.

It wasn't the grammar quiz that had my stomach in knots, though. It was thinking about our soccer game later that day—my first time back with the team since my injury. It was going to be a tough game. Even without Lisa, the Tigers were just about the best team around.

Mrs. Scott had already grabbed her red pen and started grading. We were supposed to be reading some poems in our literature book, but I couldn't concentrate.

"Hey, Arielle," Ryan Bradley whispered from his desk. "Good luck out there today. You, too, Traci. Crush those Tigers!"

Traci's cheeks turned pink. "Thanks," I whispered back.

"Arielle. Can you come here, please?" Mrs. Scott called. Oh, no. I got up and slowly approached her desk.

Mrs. Scott smiled at me kindly. "I know you've been working very hard with Amanda on your studies, and I just wanted to show you your grade."

She held up my paper. At first all I could see were red marks. But there were only about ten of them. Ten was better than twenty. Then I saw the grade: B. Okay, so it wasn't an A. But it wasn't a D, either. I was improving.

"Thanks," I said. I turned and caught Amanda's eye, and she winked back at me.

"Thank you," Mrs. Scott said. "You worked hard. Keep up the good work."

In assembly Ms. McClintic asked us to take out the questionnaires that she'd assigned to us more than two weeks ago.

"We're going to read them aloud," she announced. Oh, brother.

One by one, people stood at their desks and read from their questionnaires. I had to admit, it was actually pretty interesting getting to know new things about people in the class. One guy from Ecuador wanted to grow up to be a doctor and help people in his village back home. Another quiet girl I'd never noticed much said her favorite thing to do was feed all the animals at her uncle's farm. I was definitely going to ask her to volunteer for Healing Paws!

The shortest girl in the sixth grade, Madison Beckwith, said if she were an animal, she'd be a giraffe.

"So I could finally reach the top shelf in my locker," she said shyly.

When Ryan Bradley got to the part about what scared him most, he answered in this really quiet, serious voice, "Homeroom." Then he broke into a huge grin, and everyone laughed.

"Oh, thank you very much, Ryan," Ms. McClintic teased.

Amanda said if she were a holiday, she'd be "Easter, because it's all about spring and renewal and starting over." Cool answer. But *renewal*? That had to be a vocab word I hadn't studied.

Traci said the thing she'd most like to change about herself was "her bad fashion sense. I wish I could put stuff together the way Arielle does." She gave me a little smile. I silently promised to give her a makeover later. That is, if we both survived the Tigers match.

Then it was my turn. It was pretty weird having to say all this deep-down stuff about myself in front of my homeroom. But they were into it. They laughed at my funny answers and stayed quiet during my serious ones. I'd made it all the way through, except for one last question.

"What's the bravest thing you've ever done?" I'd written my answer a long time ago. Something about scoring a goal against this really good player at soccer camp. Suddenly it didn't feel like the right answer. Four rows of faces stared back at me, waiting for me to say something. And then it came to me.

"The bravest thing I've ever done is listen to my friends when they said I needed to change." Traci looked down at her shoes. Amanda rolled her pen on her desk. But I could feel them smiling. "And it was definitely the hardest thing I've ever done, too." Everyone was quiet. My face felt hot.

"That's all," I said, and bolted for my desk.

"Very nice, Arielle. Thank you," Ms. McClintic said quietly. "Now, who's next?"

By the end of class we all knew a lot more about one another. It had actually been pretty fun . . . for an assignment.

The bell rang, and my stomach took a dip like I was on a roller coaster. Game time.

Amanda wished me and Traci luck and put her hands on our backs "to feed our energy." It was some chakra healing thing Penny had taught her. "Felicia and I will be there cheering you on, sending you good vibes," she said. She took her hands off our backs and gave us high fives. "Go get 'em!"

In the locker room I laced up my cleats and double knotted the ends. The room was quiet, too quiet.

Sarah Johnson pulled her hair into a tight ponytail. "I am so nervous," she whispered.

She was nervous? I hadn't played in weeks. I didn't even know if my leg would hold out.

Coach Talbot blew through the locker-room doors with her clipboard in her hand. She paced around the room and began her big pep talk.

"You all know the plays. You're all good, strong players. Just remember: We play as a team. We think as a team. We will win as a team." She looked right at me. "Arielle, I know you're feeling a little rusty, but the best way to get your soccer legs again is to get right back in the game. Now, let's get out there and show those Tigers what the Muskrats are made of!"

With a little war cry we ran out on the field and warmed up. Traci gave me a thumbs-up from the sidelines. I scanned the bleachers, but I couldn't find my parents. Instead I spotted Felicia and Amanda. They saw me and started yelling and jumping up and down. It was kind of embarrassing. But where were Mom and Dad? I finally spotted them at the top of the bleachers, on their cell phones. They saw me and waved. I gave them a tiny wave back.

I scanned the Tigers' side. Lisa wasn't in the bleachers. Then I saw her, sitting with the team on the bench, her crutches propped up next to her.

Coach Talbot put her arm around my shoulders. "Arielle, don't be a hotshot out there today. Just take it easy and get comfortable in the game again. And don't forget you have teammates, okay?"

"Sure," I said. But I knew I was going to go for it. Everyone I knew was watching, and when they announced the top scorers over the loudspeaker at school tomorrow, I wanted to hear my name.

One of the refs blew the whistle, and we took our positions. Before I could even catch my breath, a tall Tiger was making her way toward me, dribbling the ball at full speed. I could do it. I could steal the ball and go for a goal. I stepped in, but she went around me easily. But I wasn't going to give up. I chased her down, stayed right by her side, and went for another steal. I put my leg out for the ball and slid, landing right on my butt. The stands erupted as the girl made a goal for the Tigers.

The whistle blew, and Coach Talbot ran out to me. "You okay, Arielle?"

I was scared to stand up, but I did.

"I'm okay, Coach."

My leg was fine. But my pride was seriously bruised,

and so was my confidence. I should have been able to make those easy plays. I had to score. I just had to.

The refs started the game again. Sarah kicked the ball, and I moved in and ran it down the field like I was on fire. I cut through the Tigers, dodging and weaving, and the next thing I knew, I kicked the ball past their goalie right into the net. The crowd went wild. I could hear Amanda and Felicia screaming my name. I was back and better than ever.

I burned up the field, trying for steals and goals. I scored again. But it wasn't enough. I wanted to win big. Sarah set up a play, but I couldn't wait. I knew I could score if I just had the ball. I went in for it and smacked into Kate Judson, one of my teammates. A Tiger girl grabbed the loose ball and scored another goal.

Kate was furious. "Hey! That was totally uncool, Arielle." She rubbed at her shin, where a big, ugly bruise was already coming up.

I couldn't believe she was mad at me. "Oh, yeah? Look, I could have scored if you hadn't been so clumsy!"

Coach Talbot stepped in between us. "Kate, take a seat and let the EMT look at that shin." The coach tapped her pen hard against her clipboard. "Arielle, you pull a stunt like that again and I will take you right out of this game."

I couldn't believe she was mad at me! "Me? She's the one who messed up," I protested.

Coach Talbot shook her head. "You're not the only

one out on that field, Arielle." She tapped her forehead with her index finger. "Use your head and play with your teammates, or I'm going to have to take you out. Traci, you sub for Kate."

I was furious, but I kept quiet. I knew I could win the game for us, but Coach Talbot was telling me to hang back. Was I the only one who wanted to win?

Sarah called us all together. "Play fifteen-A. Mina, look to me for the pass, 'kay?"

Was she kidding? Mina was the smallest player on our team.

"Okay," Mina said, looking scared.

Sarah set up the play and headed the ball to Mina. Mina missed it, and the Tigers' top scorer took off with the ball. Two seconds later she scored a goal, and the game was tied.

There were two minutes left on the clock. I could still score a goal. I just had to get the ball. Sarah ran down the field, kicking the ball. Her feet were flying. A Tiger stole it and headed the other way. Soon I was on top of her, kicking the ball out from under her and heading it back toward the goal again. Suddenly the whole Tiger team surrounded me, blocking my every move.

"Arielle!" Traci waved to me on my left. She was open. But I wanted to make the goal. I had to. I tried to make a move, but one of the tallest Tiger girls blocked my path. I had no other choice. I kicked the ball far to my left, toward Traci.

She took it and ran toward the goal. When she got close, she kicked it hard. It bounced forward and went wide. Missing the goal by a foot. The buzzer sounded. The game was over. Tigers, 3. Muskrats, 2. We'd lost. I couldn't believe it.

The next thing I knew, Coach Talbot had her arm around me.

"Great play," she said, beaming happily.

"But I didn't score. We lost. How could that be a great play?" I said.

"You played smart, not selfishly, Arielle. That's what makes a good soccer player a great one."

Traci was still standing on the messy field with her hands on her knees and her head down. I ran over and draped my arm around her shoulders. "Thanks for helping me out," I said. When she didn't respond, I added, "You did great, Traci."

Traci kept her head down. "I'm sorry, Arielle. You would have made that goal."

"Probably," I said jokingly. Traci looked up and laughed.

We walked off the field together, arm in arm. Lisa came hobbling up to meet us. "Great game, you guys. I'm looking forward to playing against you next year," she said appreciatively.

"Me too," I told her. "But next time the Muskrats are going to totally rule the Tigers."

*   *   *

135

In the locker room I packed up my gear in my back-pack and went over to Kate Judson. The bruise on her shin was dark purple. I figured she must be pretty mad at me. "Hey, Kate, I'm really sorry about what I said. And about kicking you. I hope you aren't too mad."

"No biggie," she said, smiling. "It was a pretty intense game. We've got a game against the Cougars next week. We definitely have to win that one."

"Definitely," I agreed.

That wasn't just talk. That was a promise. The whole team came over and huddled together. We held out our hands, placing them one on top of the other, and gave one last cheer.

"Go-o-o-o, *Muskrats*!" we yelled.

chapter
FIFTEEN

Things to Buy at the Mall This Weekend

Purple eye shadow

Soccer jersey from the Sports Palace

Butterfly hair clips

New Ace bandage (just in case)

Chew toys for shelter

Shauna Ferris CD case

Shauna Ferris socks

Shauna Ferris Backstage Pass videos

Don't forget to enter the Win a Chance to Meet
Shauna sweepstakes at Music Connection!

"Traci, pass the ketchup, please," I said, popping a curly french fry into my mouth.

"Where are you putting it all?" my mom asked.

"In my leg," I mumbled through a mouthful of food.

After the game Mom and Dad took the four of us

to Lulu's Family Restaurant, home of the best food in Wonder Lake—fries, burgers, and ice cream. We ordered just about everything on the menu. The waiter kept bringing out more and more. I couldn't believe how hungry I was.

Dad raised his water glass in a toast. "We are so proud of the way you girls put together that Healing Paws program at the hospital."

We all clinked glasses.

"And it will look wonderful on your college transcripts," Mom added.

I rolled my eyes. The girls tried not to laugh. "Mom, hello? College is like a million years away."

"Well," Mom said, poking at a barbecued rib. "It was still a very thoughtful and generous thing to do. Tonight you can have your Shauna CDs back."

That was the best news I'd heard all week. "Yes!" I shouted.

"So what was your favorite thing about Healing Paws?" my dad asked my friends. Oh, no, not another interrogation.

"Mine was seeing Mr. Chang talk baby talk to Grits," Felicia said. "Now I know my father's not the only one who does that."

"My favorite moment was playing with the kids," Amanda said, slurping her milk shake. "They looked like they'd completely forgotten they were in a hospital."

I thought about Jasper and Boxer. I was so glad they'd found each other.

"And the really great thing is that some of the doctors and nurses wanted to adopt pets. One of the pediatric nurses came the next day and took home two calico cats, a brother and sister," Traci told us.

"What about you, Arielle?" Felicia asked. "What was your favorite part?"

I didn't even have to think about it. "Seeing Lisa's face light up when I brought in Grits and put him on her bed," I replied.

I wanted to say more. About how good it felt to do something for someone else. It was like getting designer jeans on sale. Only much, much better.

Just then Mom's cell phone went off, and I froze. It rang again. Mom reached into her purse, picked it up, and turned it off.

"Mom," I said, totally shocked. "What if that's some important client calling from the city?"

Mom shrugged. "They can call back," she said. "Can I have the last onion ring if you're not going to eat it?"

Mom dived for the onion ring, but Dad cut her off with his fork. "Not so fast, counselor," he said, and everyone laughed.

"Oh, my gosh, Asher Bank is sitting two tables over—don't look!" Felicia squealed.

Of course we all looked.

"Who's Asher Bank?" Dad asked, way too loud.

"Shhhhhh!" we all said at once.

"He's the president of student government," Felicia said quietly, like that explained everything. She left out the part about Asher being really cute.

"Who's he with?" Amanda asked.

I recognized a few of the kids. They were all eighth graders. Most of them had been in the auditorium the day I'd hidden in there to escape from Coach Talbot. That day seemed so far away now.

"Why don't you go talk to him?" I couldn't resist teasing Amanda. Her cheeks broke out in red splotches.

"Why don't *you* go talk to him?" she said back. "I dare you."

"I double dare you," I answered.

"Oh, yeah? Well . . ." She trailed off, and I saw why. Asher and his friends were leaving. And they were coming straight toward our table on their way to the door! Asher looked unbelievably cute in his navy blue sweater and jeans, his short hair kind of spiked up and messy.

Asher stopped at our table. "Hi," he said. He looked at Amanda. "You're Amanda Kempner, right?"

"Right," she croaked.

"I got your application for student government. I'm glad you're going to join us. See you Monday," he said, and walked out with his friends.

"Oh, my gosh. Tell me I don't have ketchup all over my face," Amanda said.

"Just on your mouth." I shrugged.

"So do you!" Amanda said, pointing to my face.

We laughed so hard, people started staring at our table. Mom tried to keep a straight face and pretend everything was normal.

"We're acting so totally fifth grade," I said, wiping tears from my eyes.

The waiter cleared our table and brought us dessert menus. "Dessert, anyone?" he asked.

"Definitely," I said. My eyes scanned the menu. Mud pie, strawberry shortcake, hot fudge brownie sundae, blueberry cobbler, various ice cream sundaes.

"What are you getting?" Felicia asked, reading over my shoulder.

The last thing on the menu was Lulu's giant ice cream sundae: eight scoops of ice cream, fresh strawberries and bananas, nuts, and hot fudge. There was a message written underneath the description of the sundae: *Your friends are you're greatest possessions. Hold on to them forever.*

I looked up and smiled at the waiter. "May I please have the giant ice cream sundae?" I told him.

"Arielle," Mom cried. "You can't possibly eat all that!"

"And four spoons," I added.

The menu lay on the table in front of me. I read

the quote again: *Your friends are you're greatest posses-sions. Hold on to them forever.*

"Hey," I said, picking it up. "They got it wrong."

Amanda looked confused. "What do you mean?"

"See? They spelled it *you're* instead of *your. You are* instead of the possessive *your.* The grammar's wrong."

"Quick, call Mrs. Scott and tell her the news!" Traci joked.

"You could bring it to class for extra credit," Felicia added.

Amanda pulled a pen out of her bag and scribbled *A+* on my paper napkin. "There's hope for you yet, Arielle Davis," she said.

"Yeah, right," I said, tucking my hair behind my ear and smiling despite myself.

Whatever.